DECORATION DAY

BY VIC KERRY

The woman looked toward him, then back down at the headstone. David took a step toward her. As he watched, she evaporated into violet mist. He rubbed his eyes and blinked as hard as he could. Nothing of the woman remained. David began to think that he was hallucinating. The stress of everything had to be getting to him. To indulge his curiosity, he walked to the headstone. It looked as old as many of the others, but the letters etched into the rock had held up better than most. He recognized the name, but the date bothered him. It read Louisa Marsh, 1832–1864, Beloved wife and mother. David glanced at the smaller stone beside Louisa's grave marker. The fading words said Henry Marsh, 1856–1864.

He looked up at the church. Once again, the purple flame moved around the sanctuary past the windows. Someone definitely carried it this time. The woman in black who had disappeared at the grave moved back and forth, waving the hideous light as if to tempt David back into the building. The preacher ran inside, trampling his sermon underfoot as he passed. The woman carried an invisible candle topped by the purple flame.

"What is this?" he yelled at her.

She came toward him, bearing the candle ahead. The black veil obscured her face, and she said nothing.

"In the name of all that is holy in this house of God, what are you?" David yelled.

The flame flickered out, but the woman kept coming closer. He could almost touch her. When she drew close enough, David grabbed hold of her veil and pulled it down. The fabric slipped away from her face.

Instead of a human visage or even a skull, a horrible mass of entwined, squirming, tentacle-like projections reached out from where the face should have been. They groped for him. He let go of the veil and stumbled backward. Terror like he never felt before engulfed him. His feet slipped on the hardwood floor, and he toppled, hitting his head on the edge of a pew. His world didn't go dark, but lilac.

DEDICATION

This one is for the beta readers: Laura and Lauren.

SUNDAY AFTERNOON

David stood in front of the wrought-iron gates of a stone church building. He'd been driving down a narrow mountain road when it widened out and the church appeared out of the afternoon fog. Water dripped from tree limbs hanging over a stone and iron fence that encircled the structure. Cold droplets fell on David's shoulder.

Something from deep inside his soul tugged at him, like a feeling the building beckoned him. David's life had been meaningless for such a long time. Now this place called him. David stepped back from the gates to take in the whole vista of the place.

Just beyond the fence, tilted, lichen-covered gravestones stretched out across the churchyard all the way to the foundations of the building. A narrow path paved with flat rocks led to the church door, and it was the only area in the yard devoid of headstones. The church sat on high limestone foundations that looked as if they had been hand hewn. The building was made of smaller, similarly hewn blocks. The roof pitched sharply, and slate shingles lay askew on it. A metal steeple ascended into the air. A strange star topped the spire.

David noticed the gates had a similar design worked into the metal—a ball with twisting arms radiating from it. He'd never seen anything like it on a church, and that fascinated him more. God told him this was the place for him to start his new flock. Never had the call to preach been so strong. He had to learn more about the building.

David got back into his car and continued down the winding road. A town would be close. The church and its grounds were too well kept to be abandoned. No one would travel this secluded, off-the-main-drag road he was on without living nearby. David ventured on only because of the strange stirrings sent from God and sheer wanderlust, which had been the main thing driving him since the death of his beloved wife more than a year ago.

Rain began to fall as he drove farther down the side of the mountain. The black pavement bore no painted lines. As the rain became steadier, David had a tougher time staying on his side of the road. That didn't worry him much because he'd not met a single vehicle since starting down the mountain.

He thought of the poem by Robert Frost. Oftentimes the best things lay at the end of the road less taken. The fog dissipated, but the relentlessness of the rain made it almost impossible to see more than a few feet ahead. David focused hard on the road. It was like driving down a waterfall. He tapped the brakes to slow his descent. The rear of the car swayed back and forth. He let off the brake and allowed the car to coast down the hill, giving it no gas and staying in the middle to keep from accidentally going over the side.

Lightning flashed. David waited for the thunder but heard none. Another flash of lightning, and again no thunder. And then the next flash of lightning almost blinded him, and thunder like a train's air horn deafened him.

Suddenly, David realized a truck was racing toward him. He'd concentrated so hard on the road directly in front of him that he'd failed to notice he was about to be hit head-on. The air horn sounded again, and he swerved back to his side of the road. His car skidded and skimmed across flowing water. The tires sank into the soft earth on a very narrow shoulder that sloped into a ravine off the side of the mountain. David somehow was able to look over the edge at his impending doom and, at what seemed like at the same time, see the oncoming vehicle. An ancient truck, maybe fifty years old, pulling an old tanker trailer rumbled past.

The wooded slope to the ravine glowed green despite the heavy rain. As if doing so on its own, David's car avoided rolling to the bottom of the hollow and also avoided colliding with the tanker. As his foot hovered over the brake pedal, the road flattened out into a valley. The rain slacked off as he passed an old wooden sign, leaning and proclaiming in peeling letters, *Welcome to Innsboro, Tennessee. Population: 375.* A small town divided by a little creek lay not far down the road. Everything looked gray. David didn't know if it was caused by the heavily overcast sky or if the town was really that dim.

As he drove into the town, the streets became inlaid brick. The car bounced over the uneven surface. A few streets crisscrossed the main drag. David looked down one that crossed the creek. A service station sat on the opposite bank. He turned down that street. Steel girders that rose into the air, leveled off and went back down again framed the one-lane bridge. The pavement smoothed out as he drove across the bridge. The street became brick again on the other side of the creek.

The town looked abandoned, as did the service station. David parked, blocking the gas pumps. He got out of his car, and a fine mist dampened him as he walked to the glass doors of the service station. He stepped inside.

The air in the building smelled stale and a little bit like mold. A fluorescent lamp hummed overhead, casting its green light over the place. An old-fashioned vending machine sat in the corner. The formerly vibrant red of the Coca-Cola advertisement had seen better decades. A counter sat against the far wall, beside a swinging door that apparently led to the garage. Nothing sat on the counter, not even a cash register. The wire racks below it were empty except for a few wax-paper-wrapped tubes of Necco Wafers and three extra-long Tootsie Rolls. It was like being in an episode of *The Twilight Zone.*

"Hello?" David called out.

Something crashed behind the swinging door. It startled him. He hadn't expected an answer.

"Hello? I've got a question," he said when no one came from the back.

The door swung open, and a squat man with bulging eyes and pasty skin stepped through. He wore greasy, gray coveralls and held a ratchet in his hand. The attendant, whose name patch read "Thomas," stared David up and down.

"Maybe you could help me," David said.

The squat man shrugged his shoulders and curled his lip. "What?"

The attendant even sounded like a toad when he croaked his answer. It took a minute for David to gather himself to make his inquiry. "I saw a church up the road just a bit, and I wondered if anyone still goes there."

"Yeah."

"Frequently?"

Thomas looked him up and down again. "Who wants to know?"

David was glad the man could speak more than a few words. "I do. I'm a preacher or was a preacher. I feel that God has called me to preach there."

"Mr. Marsh," Thomas said, turning to go back to the garage. "I don't understand. What do you mean by that?"

The squat man turned back to David. He huffed and rolled his watery eyes. "You need to talk to Mr. Marsh."

"Excellent. Where is he?"

"Up the hill in the big house."

Thomas didn't wait for anything else. He slunk into the garage, leaving the swinging door doing just that, and David standing rather confused. He shook his head and walked back to his car. The mist had let up, and a slip of sunshine came through the clouds. In the fresh light of the sun, the town looked grayer than it had in the rain.

He drove back across the bridge and stayed on that street because it ran up the side of the mountain. A few stores lined the way. They all looked abandoned, but then the gas station had as well. David thought perhaps a few of them might still be in business. As he started up the hill, he passed a small café. There were people sitting at a table by the window. They all eyed him as he passed. He could feel them staring at him more than see them. The town must not get many visitors.

Houses lined the street as it wound up the hill. Most were small cottages with wooden siding with peeled paint. At the top of the street, the land flattened out on a large, constructed terrace. To the side, a house towered between old, gnarled oak trees. A wrought-iron fence encompassed it like the one at the church. A gate allowed access from the street. The house's foundation looked like that of the church, but the rest was made of gray siding like the other houses. It stood three stories. A porch wrapped around the entire lower floor. French doors on the second story opened onto a small veranda that made up part of the porch's ceiling. In its day, the house would have been a marvelous plantation home. A weathervane that looked like the symbol on the church's steeple turned in the wind.

David parked his car on the curb beside the house. He climbed out and walked to the gate. Water splattered him from the looming old oak trees. It felt like the rain hadn't stopped. David felt a chill, which had nothing to do with the weather, shiver through him.

The gate opened with little effort. David walked up to the house. The floorboards of the porch bowed from years of exposure to the humidity. He tripped over one as he walked to the door, but his shoulder hit the heavy oak frame before his face hit the ground. The impact caused the clapper in a bell hanging from the knocker to clang. David steadied himself. Before he could ring the bell again, the door creaked open.

A short woman with a pronounced hump on her back looked up at him. She wore a light gray dress with a white apron. Her hair was under a gray cap, and her skin almost matched it in color. Her eyes bulged out at him, large and watery. She looked like a slightly feminine version of the gas station attendant.

"What?" she croaked.

"I was told that Mr. Marsh lives here. Is that true?"

"Why?"

David took a deep breath. "I wanted to talk to him about the church up the road."

"Thank you, Thomasine; that will be enough," a deep, smooth voice said from the gloom of the house.

The maid shrugged her shoulders and moved out of the way. A tall man wearing a deep red robe trimmed in black velvet stepped into the light. His face had sharp, angular features with a beaked nose. His jet-black hair hung midway down his neck. He had the bangs shoved behind his ears. His eyes pierced David to the core.

"How can I help you?" he asked with his silky voice.

"Are you Mr. Marsh?"

"Indeed. And you are?"

David stuck his hand out. "I'm Reverend David Stanley."

Marsh took his hand. Marsh's felt chilled but firm. "Delighted to meet you, Reverend Stanley. Won't you please come in?"

David followed Marsh into the foyer. The door closed behind him. Its thud echoed through the house. The entranceway was tiled with slate like the shingles at the church. A large mirror in an ornate silver frame hung on the wall. It caught some of the sunlight filtering through the windows, casting a dim light over everything.

"Please excuse my maid. We don't get very many visitors." Marsh pointed toward another room with a flourish of his hand. "Most people don't even know we're here."

David followed his host. "This certainly is off the beaten path. I just happened upon the road and wondered what was at the end."

"Isn't that the way most great experiences occur?" Marsh said, stopping in a well-lighted sitting room.

He sat in a high-backed chair cushioned in crimson velvet. Another flourish of his hand offered David a seat on the equally lush sofa.

"I'll get to the point, Mr. Marsh. I was wondering if that church just up the road has a minister."

Marsh reclined into the richness of his chair and interlocked his fingers. "You are interested in our little church house?"

"Yes," David replied as he remained perched on the edge of the couch. The cushions sank down a little more than he liked.

"Why?"

"I have been a reverend for thirty years. I left my congregation after my wife of nearly as long passed away. I felt listless and useless. I've been wandering around ever since."

"I know the sense of listlessness you experience upon the death of a wife. My dear Louisa has been dead many years," Marsh said softly. "I haunted the halls of this house many months with no repose."

"I am sorry for your loss," David said.

"And I yours. Wives should be a once-in-a-lifetime experience. It's enough to destroy your entire life when they are gone," Marsh said. "Is that the experience you had?"

"Until I saw that church, Mr. Marsh."

"Please, we are brothers in widowhood. Call me Alistair."

"Alistair, when I saw that church, God spoke to me. He said that I need to be the preacher there and bring his glory to it."

"Reverend Stanley."

"Please, call me David."

"Yes, David. Are you sure that it wasn't your own conscience that told you that, instead of the Almighty?"

David shook his head. "Have you ever had a calling from God?"

Marsh made a steeple with his fingers and smiled, showing small, square teeth. "I cannot say that I have."

"I have twice before. This was exactly like those times. God wants me to preach there. He needs me to. I need to. I need meaning in my life, Alistair."

"We are currently without a minister." Marsh leaned forward. "You have to understand that we are a small community and an equally small congregation. We cannot pay you much."

"I understand. I'll work for enough to feed myself and pay rent, unless there is a parsonage."

"The last minister lived in the church. There is a small apartment in the back. Just a sitting area with a bed, small kitchen and bathroom. Nothing refined."

"Sounds good."

Marsh nodded. "I will need to talk to a few of the elders, but I think we can arrange something." He stood. "Get a few of your belongings from your car. You will sleep here tonight, and tomorrow, if the elders agree, we will go to the church."

"I don't want to inconvenience you. I can stay at a motel."

Marsh laughed. It sounded like a hollow echo in a mountain cave. "We don't have any inns or motels. Don't let the name of the town fool you."

"I suppose I will impose myself on your kindness then," David said.

"No imposition at all. I'll have Thomasine prepare a guest

room for you." Marsh turned to walk out of the room, stopped and said, "Let me give you some advice though. This is an old house. Don't go poking around where you shouldn't. You might not like what you find."

MONDAY

An old-fashioned alarm clock ticked against the silence of the bedroom. The monotonous sound should have lulled him to sleep, but the noise the clock produced sounded less like the ticking of a metronome and more like the beating of heart. David put a pillow over his head to help muffle the ticking, but that only made the sound more like a heartbeat.

Bedsprings poked him in the back through a thin mattress on the single bed frame. He rolled onto his side. One of the coiled metal devils poked him right in the ribs. David sat up, planting his feet on the oiled wooden floor. The clock beat on. Enough moonlight filtered in through the windows for him to see the time: three o'clock. Apparently, he'd slept some without realizing it, because he'd gone to bed sometime after supper, around eleven o'clock.

Thomasine had left a crystal pitcher filled with water on the dresser across the room. David walked to it. The floorboards creaked as he did so. They moaned as if under extreme agony. He wondered how long it had been since someone slept in the room that was his for the night. Although the room was rather large, the bed was reminiscent of those he'd seen while touring a closed convent.

He poured some water in a cut-glass goblet beside the pitcher on the tray. The lukewarm water didn't refresh him, but it did quench his thirst. The dust and stuffy air of the room messed with his sinuses.

I suppose Marsh doesn't want me to be too comfortable.

David left the light off but looked around the room. It was strange how much light seeped in. The moon must be full, and the sky clear, although he remembered it had started raining before he'd gone to bed. An old sofa sat against the wall under a window. It looked more comfortable than the bed. David grabbed a quilt from the mattress and lay down on the plush sofa. His feet didn't hang off the end. No springs poked him, and the cushions gave him just enough support.

As he tried to ignore the ceaseless beating of the Baby Ben clock, he lifted the gauzy curtain to stare at the night sky. Rain pattered on the windowpane.

"Where is the light coming from?" he wondered, lying back on the arm of the sofa. Purple light seeped from the cracks between the crown molding and the ceiling.

David blinked hard and even rubbed his eyes, not believing what he saw. When he looked again, the light was there. That light—not the moon—lit the room. As the clock ticked, the light pulsed just enough to be visible. He blinked again, thinking that it was a trick of his eyes. But when he paid closer attention, he saw that the light indeed dimmed and brightened in sync with the clock.

David got up again and went to the door. The old brass handle felt cool in his hand as he turned it. Although Marsh had told him not to wander around the house after bedtime, he had to know what was going on. He stepped into the hallway lighted by an ornate electric sconce. Nothing seemed out of place. Old paintings of seascapes and rocky beaches hung on the wall. An elaborate piece of furniture like a buffet stood between two doors opposite his. David assumed they too led to unused bedrooms. He looked at the ceiling. No purple light filtered down. He peeked back into his own room. The light still pulsated softly. Something was happening above his room.

He walked down the hallway toward the staircase. A runner muffled his footfalls, but an occasional floorboard moaned as if tattle-telling on him. He thought about tiptoeing. The whole thing felt very childish—like he'd watched a scary movie that wouldn't let him sleep. It felt like an Edgar Allen Poe story. He hoped that a raven didn't accost him on the way to the third floor. David thought that a ghost might even cross his path.

Before his wife died, he never would have thought such

things. People died, and their spirits either went to the paradise of Abraham's bosom or the everlasting torment of the pit. Nothing lingered between worlds. But after his beloved— Anna—suffered for so long despite his fervent prayers, he didn't know what he believed. His uncertainty about things, especially spiritual, drove him away from the church on his long soul-searching trip, if there was a soul.

Now he topped the last stair to the third floor of the old home. The third-floor hallway was lit in a soft, glowing violet light. The source of it seemed to come from behind a closed door midway down the hall. The thin light gave the whole scene a dim, tainted appearance. No furniture lined the hall. Only candle sconces hung from the walls. This part of the house seemed devoid of electricity. The carpet looked more worn than any in the rest of the house. Many feet had passed over it many times. David followed in the unseen footsteps as he made his way to the mysterious door.

The handle was not brass but glass. The beveling on it made it feel like a giant jewel. It turned, but the door would not budge. David looked at the handle. Amethyst light shone through a keyhole. He'd never peeked through one of these, but he had to know what was in the room.

Just like in every old, scary movie he'd ever seen, the keyhole revealed what was on the other side of the locked door. There seemed to be no source for the light, but he saw an empty room with a large portrait hanging on the opposite wall. The painting looked like Alistair Marsh, but the dress appeared much older, Civil War era perhaps. People or things seemed to be standing behind him. David couldn't make it out through such a small peephole.

"I thought I told you not to wander around the halls at night," Marsh said from behind him.

David jumped to his feet. His heart beat much faster than the alarm clock in his room could. He turned to his host, who was dressed in a red silk robe and holding a candle in a candlestick.

"I couldn't sleep because a purple light shined into my room. It was coming from up here. I came to see if I could put it out."

The flickering candlelight played on the angles of Marsh's

face. He looked sinister with deep shadows on his cheeks and eyes.

"I don't see any light," he said.

David looked down. No light seeped from the crack at the bottom of the door. "It was just there. I even saw a picture of one of your ancestors hanging on the wall."

Marsh shook his head. "We don't use this floor of the house. It's never even been wired for electricity. I think maybe you were dreaming and perhaps sleepwalked up here. Let me take you back to your room."

"I've never sleepwalked before," David said. "Things seem so real."

"Sometimes old houses can do strange things to people." Marsh put his hand on David's shoulder. "That is the reason I warned you to be careful of this place."

"I really don't think I was dreaming. I have no idea why I would concoct such a dream."

"Tomorrow, when you are rested and the sun is up, I will show you that nothing is in that room and dispel your doubts that you were just dreaming."

David nodded his agreement and followed Marsh back to his room. As he lay down on the sofa, no purple light seeped from the cracks in the ceiling. He heard Marsh lock his door and hoped his host only did it out of worry. He had had nightmares since Anna died, but never walked around the house in his sleep. The locked door scared him too. Marsh was a stranger, even if he had been hospitable. David decided to wait and see what happened.

He closed his eyes and listened to the tick-tock of the Baby Ben. It sounded like a clock again, not a heartbeat. Everything had been only a dream.

Just before he drifted off to sleep, David thought he heard footsteps on the floor above him. Had someone entered the empty room? He tried to rouse himself, but sleep had become too irresistibly strong.

The creaking of the bedroom door awakened David. He sat up to see Thomasine walking in with a tray. She walked across to him and started to lay it across his lap. The tray was wider than the sofa. She glared at him.

"Sorry," he said, slinging his legs around and sitting properly on the sofa. "I could've come down for breakfast. There was no need for such formality."

"No formality. The master always eats in bed. All the guests do as well."

Before she could sit the tray on his lap, David caught the corner. "What is breakfast?"

She glowered at him. "Porridge, melba toast, marmalade, and kipper with coffee."

"I think I'd rather not," he said. The sound of the breakfast put a brick in his stomach. "I'll just take the coffee."

David took the china teacup from the tray. Thomasine looked disgusted and started out of the room. She stopped by the dresser and placed the water pitcher and glass on the tray. She slammed the door.

He felt a bit of relief that the unpleasant maid was gone and took a swig of coffee. The unexpected bitterness of chicory nearly made him spew it on the floor. Fortunately, the liquid was tepid enough for him to swallow it before making a mess or burning his gullet out.

David walked to the dresser and left the coffee there. Thomasine had said that Marsh took his breakfast in bed. This might be the best opportunity for David to sneak up to the third floor and look back into that room. Now that morning had broken, he knew he wasn't dreaming or sleepwalking, despite what Marsh had said.

David went to the small carpet bag he'd brought up from his car the night before. He kept a change of clothes and pajamas in it so he didn't have to unload his entire car when he'd stopped for the night during his wanderings. The toilet kit came in handy. A quick shave with his electric razor while looking in a small hand mirror cleaned him up enough as did hitting his hair a lick with his travel brush. David changed into a pair of black slacks and blue long-sleeved shirt. The top of his white undershirt peeked out from the open button at the neck. He felt he was ready to investigate what he'd dreamt last night.

The hallway was empty when he crept into it. In the morning light, the corridor looked a little livelier, but still felt heavy and sullen. He eased down the hall, back to the staircase. Everything was as he remembered it from the night before.

Pans clattered from the main floor. David paused midstep. He heard Thomasine cursing and could tell she was well beneath him. After a few more eternal seconds, he started up the stairs.

At the landing, things looked different than they had last night. Heavy tapestries draped the walls, covering where the candle sconces would have been. The fabrics lay flat against the wall with no sign of a bulge that would have denoted hidden fixtures. A large candle chandelier hung from the middle of the ceiling.

David looked at each tapestry as he walked down the hall. They all depicted ocean scenes. A schooner broke up on rocks on the first hanging. The next showed dark, bent figures emerging from the frothy waves. He stopped at where the door to the mysterious room was supposed to be. A tapestry hung there. David pressed his hand against it. Solid wall backed the hanging. He pushed the edge aside and found that a wall was indeed behind the hanging.

The tapestry dropped back in place as he let it go. The picture woven into the cloth was another maritime vignette. A schooner tossed up on fitful waves. The sky behind it glowed purple. It actually seemed to glow. David touched the stitching. It felt coarse like the rest of the thread used in the hanging.

"Trying to see if you were indeed dreaming?" Marsh said from behind David.

He started and turned around. His host stood with his arms crossed and a bemused expression on his face. David smiled.

"It seemed so real," he said. "I couldn't believe that it wasn't."

"I told you that this is an old house and many dreams and nightmares float around its halls." Marsh flourished his hand toward the stairs. "My car is waiting to take us to the church. The other elders are meeting us there."

David walked toward the stairs. "You aren't mad at me?"

"Curiosity is a powerful thing, Reverend Stanley. I cannot

fault you for that. I probably would have investigated myself."

They walked down the stairs. David passed the second floor and headed to ground level. "It killed the cat, though."

Marsh laughed. It was a pleasant sound. "True. Fortunately, you aren't one."

They stepped onto the hardwood of the ground floor. Marsh led David through the kitchen to the back door. They went outside. A fine mist washed over David's skin as they walked to an idling Lincoln Continental that had been around at least since the Nixon presidency. The black paint looked showroom-floor fresh, however. The squat man from the gas station walked around the car and opened the door for Marsh, who sat down in the backseat. Thomas—David remembered the name from the patch on the attendant's uniform—closed the door. He walked back to the driver's side. David walked around and got in the back with Marsh.

Black leather covered the bench seat. Marsh stared straight ahead as the car began to roll. A piece of glass separated the driver from the passenger compartment. David had seen something like that only in movie limousines.

"This is a very nice car," he said, mostly to make small talk.

"Yes. Thomas keeps it in fine condition. I'd hate to buy a new one." Marsh never looked at David.

"Thomas works for you too?"

"You know Thomas?"

"I stopped in at the gas station yesterday. He's the one who gave me directions to your house."

Marsh nodded. "His family has been servants to my family for centuries."

"Centuries?"

The other man finally looked at him. His eyes studied him. "Yes."

"You don't find that weird?"

A disquieting smile stretched across Marsh's lips again. "Not really. It is our way in this town. We keep the old traditions and hold family very important."

"To the point of keeping families as servants?"

"Yes. Thomas's family came over from England as servants to

the Marshes. When we moved from New England to Tennessee, the tradition continued. It helped to keep us from that horrible exercise of slavery that destroyed so many powerful families."

David looked out the window as they passed through the town. A few people walked the broken sidewalks in the misty morning. Most looked short and stocky like Thomas and Thomasine. The small café served a few of the dumpy people. The car turned and headed up the mountain toward the church.

"Everyone looks alike," David said without thinking.

"Only the servants. They marry within themselves, so there are a lot of similarities. You will notice that none of the elders look alike."

"Is the town population just your servants?"

"We have few outsiders now that the road has been all but forgotten." Marsh looked out the window into the swirling fog. "It is better that way. My beloved Louisa was an outsider. She came to an unfortunate end."

"Do you mean that she was murdered?"

"No."

David wished that he hadn't come to the town, but when they stopped before the church building, he felt the tug of God's hand on his heartstrings. His faith seemed to fill him again when he saw the place. A few men dressed in raincoats and large-brimmed hats milled around the graveyard. Despite what Marsh had said, they all looked very much like soggy brown sacks.

"The elders," Marsh said as Thomas opened the door. "They are checking on their ancestors. It is something we love doing. Our past is very important to us."

Marsh stepped into the mist. David got out of the car and walked to meet him at the opened gate. They walked in side by side. The other men turned as soon as they crossed into the churchyard as if the elders had sensed them crossing that line.

"Gentlemen, may I present to you Reverend David Stanley? He wishes to pastor our congregation," Marsh said.

The first elder walked to him. Beady eyes stared from under the brim of the hat. A piggy nose that showed too much nostril turned up to David. The second elder stepped over, examining him from behind round glasses perched on a thin nose. All took their turns looking him over.

"I am Horace Stovall," the pig-nosed elder said.

"My name is Ebenezer Hollingsworth," Eyeglasses said.

"Dmitri Covington," the third, bland-looking elder said.

"I am Nahum Fernwell," the final elder said.

Of all the elders Nahum appeared the oldest, but with the garb the men wore, it was hard to tell.

"I have made the reverend aware of a few things, like the importance of family, but I have left everything else to be discussed today," Marsh said.

"How did you gentlemen get here?" David asked.

They all looked at each other as if they had been asked the dumbest question imaginable.

"They were driven here by their drivers, just like us." Marsh pointed to the road. The Lincoln was gone. "The road is not wide enough for our cars to stay parked on the shoulders. A gas tanker is due any time now. We wouldn't want our cars or gasoline destroyed."

"I understand. I met the truck when I came in yesterday. It was an antique."

The elders murmured to themselves. He didn't like the sound. They seemed bothered. David decided he needed to be more careful if he was to get the pastorship of the church.

"Since you hold family in such high honor, I think that the first thing I should do for services Sunday is have a decoration," he said. "Why not celebrate the deceased by making this cemetery look beautiful?"

"Ancestors," Horace stated. "They are not deceased."

"I'm sorry," David said. "We can still celebrate their lives by decorating their graves."

"Markers," Nahum said. "Graves are for the dead. These are our ancestors."

David had no idea what these men meant. All the headstones he'd glanced at so far had birth and death dates on them. He would play along. God pulled so hard on his will he thought he might pass out from the overwhelming desire. He stepped onto the entrance stoop.

"I would like to see inside," he said.

"I don't recall a minister so excited about our faith," Dmitri said. "Ever."

"God has called to me about this place and this church." David looked at the elder. "I've been struggling with my faith for a long time. This place revives it."

"So he knows nothing about our ways?" Dmitri asked Marsh.

"I plan on talking to him after he sees our church," Marsh said. "I'm sure his enthusiasm won't have waned after that."

The conversation between the two men piqued David's interest. Something seemed off about it. He wondered if they practiced some strange version of Christianity. Perhaps they handled snakes. He didn't like the idea of that but felt he could convince them that it was better to handle metaphorical serpents. He noticed that the elders spoke and held themselves better than the other townspeople.

Marsh stepped past him, carrying a large iron key in his hand. He unlocked the door and swung it open. The heavy iron hinges ground together with teeth-jarring metal on metal sound. A rush of stale air hit David in the face as he walked inside.

A very small vestibule gave way to the sanctuary. Small, solid oak pews lined a narrow aisle. The space between pews left little room for legs if the people were as tall as Marsh. David ran his hand over the smooth, oiled wood of each bench as he passed.

The only light in the room came from the leaded windows, but a large candle chandelier hung from the ceiling about where the spire steeple jutted from the roof. He figured that the metal spire helped to hold up the chandelier.

"How do you light the candles?" he asked, staring at the chandelier in wonder.

"With a long match," Nahum said, obviously as a joke, but sounding devoid of humor.

"We have an altar boy for that," Marsh said.

David looked at him. "So this is a Catholic church."

"Not exactly," Dmitri said.

"Episcopal?"

"Not that either," Horace said.

"We have our own altar boys. We don't hold to an orthodox faith," Marsh said. "After you've had time to settle in, I will educate you on the esoteric nature of our faith."

David's jolliness wavered. "I don't know if I can satisfy your needs. I have a very specific form of preaching. It might not match yours if your faith strays far from mine."

"You should have vetted him," Dmitri said.

"Perhaps you would like to be the minister with Decoration Day so near," Marsh said. "You are the most versed in Scripture, Dmitri."

"No," the other man answered.

Marsh looked at David. The gaze provided no comfort. "I have total confidence in your abilities, Reverend."

"So you like the idea of a decoration day?" he asked.

"Believe it or not, our decoration day is this Sunday every year," Ebenezer broke his silence. "We were afraid that we might not have a preacher for it."

"How lucky I happened upon your town when I did," David said. "God works in mysterious ways."

"Indeed he does," Marsh said. "Let's continue the tour."

Marsh walked past David, directing his attention to the pulpit. Carved vines snaked the sides of the oak podium. Tiny spikes like briar thorns jutted from the carvings. David imagined they represented the thorns used to make Christ's crown. Now that he thought about the symbol on the steeple, he imagined it represented the Star of Bethlehem. The people of this congregation might believe in celebrating the birth more than the death of Christ, which he could work with. The fears of having to dance holding a copperhead began to fade.

They passed the pulpit and stared down a short stack of steps. A large, open vat sat beside them. David looked into it, expecting to see water, but instead saw deep blackness.

"Is that the baptistery?" he asked.

"No; it is the pit," Marsh said as if that made sense.

"Pit to what?" David asked.

"To the unknowable," Nahum said.

David took those words and placed them into his memory. Tonight he would have to mull that over to figure out what it meant. The elders liked to be cryptic, and he was sure that this wouldn't be explained. He was correct.

"Let me show you into the parson's apartment," Marsh said. He pushed a recessed wooden panel. It swung open to reveal a cramped vault room.

A wooden stove sat in the corner. A cot-like bed was on the opposite wall. Under a small, round window sat a table that probably doubled as a desk. A short bookshelf hid behind the door. A door near the bed had a crescent moon cut out of it. He assumed this was the bathroom.

"So I live in the church?"

"Most holy men like to be cloistered near their workplaces," Horace said.

"A parsonage is just a larger version," Dmitri said.

"Is there electricity?"

Marsh flipped a switch. A single bulb hanging from the middle of the sloped ceiling chased away only a small amount of the gloom. David noticed there wasn't a refrigerator in the room—only a small pie safe.

"How about food storage?" he asked.

"We will get you an icebox," Nahum said. "The last minister stole the one from here."

"Stole?"

"He wasn't well suited for us," Ebenezer said. "I am sure you will do better. You already seem more enthusiastic than he was."

"We will leave you here," Marsh said. "I think that you will want to familiarize yourself with the building and grounds. I will send a basket of food to you later. Tomorrow I will send the car to bring you to my house. We will discuss the preparations for Sunday."

Before David could say anything, the elders left him in his small cell. They never looked back as they left the church.

David walked back into the sanctuary. The vat called *the pit* worried him. He wondered if that was where the congregation kept their snakes. Enough light came into the church that he could see into the vat for a ways. Nothing slithered. He hoped that the altar boy wasn't responsible for stocking the thing. David fished a penny out of his pocket and tossed it over the side of the pit. It never clattered on the bottom or if it did, the pit was so deep that it muffled the sound. David felt as if the walls of the building were closing in, and everything seemed very heavy.

He decided to go back to his apartment and look over the books on the shelf. Maybe they would explain something about the town's religious practices. He was still examining things when Thomas delivered a large meal about three in the afternoon and departed without a word.

As night fell, David discovered the sermon diary of the last minister at the church. He sat in a straight chair at the desk and opened the book. A sermon outline would certainly aid him in ministering to the people of Innsboro. The first sermon in the book was dated one year ago on the upcoming Sunday. The header read *Decoration Day,* with a heavy pencil line under those words. The sermon outline followed that. The previous minister had chosen to preach about the exodus of the Israelites to the Promised Land. The former minister framed it as their homecoming.

David liked the outline, so he wanted to see what further musings he might find for his own use. He flipped the page. It was blank. All the rest were the same. Apparently the former minister had taken his other sermon outlines with him like he supposedly had the refrigerator.

TUESDAY

Anna stood at the foot of David's bed. She smiled at him like she always had. He hadn't dreamed about her in a very long time. Only then, it was when his mind was troubled. Perhaps she could provide him some guidance on what he should preach for his first sermon in Innsboro.

"Why are you here?" he asked her.

She opened her arms wide and flourished her hands. He waited for an answer, but all she did was repeat the same movements with her hands, over and over.

"I don't understand. Can't you speak?"

Anna put her finger to her lips, the universal sign to be quiet. She pointed at the door to the church. David got out of bed. He walked to his dream wife and reached out to touch her. His fingers felt her skin, cold and clammy. He tried to grasp her. She pulled away and waggled her finger at him, shaking her head.

"Is this a dream?"

She made that sweeping motion with her hand toward the door. Now he noticed it. The same violet light that had seeped into his room at Marsh's mansion filtered in around the church door. It pulsed from a dim light to a brighter one, something like a flickering neon sign. He stepped toward it. Anna grabbed his arm and pulled him to her. She shook her head again.

"I dreamed about that light at Marsh's house last night," he said to her. "I want to see what it is."

Her fingernails dug into his arm. David felt it, even in his dream state. He couldn't remember feeling anything during a dream. Thinking he would awaken from this dream, David realized that was not the case—nothing happened. He pulled away from his wife and walked to the door. The doorknob felt warm and vibrated with energy when he touched it. Anna touched his shoulder and tried to pull him back, but he moved away.

As he walked into the church, the purple light filled the whole place. Everything glowed with it. He stepped deeper inside his church.

"No," Anna said.

David turned to look at his wife. She charged after him. Anna crossed the threshold between the apartment and the church, and as David reached out to her, she disintegrated into a million misty particles. The light began to blink in and out. The room went dark. The violet light flared. It blinded him. When the room darkened again, his vision carried with it the afterglow. Everything looked as if it were under a black light. Any light color, like his white T-shirt that peeked from last button of his shirt, glowed. He started to the steps into the sanctuary. The pit caught his attention.

Waves of energy seemed to rise from it. His changed vision helped him see it. They were small and barely visible. He even thought they made a slight humming noise. A burst of purple light erupted from the pit. It shot straight into the air and appeared to pass through the ceiling.

He heard the sound of rain on the roof. David hurried up the steps to the sanctuary and peered out of the window. Drops of violet light hit the ground and streaked the old glass. The streaking color ran together and began to form words. He had never seen anything like it.

His vision blurred as if he needed reading glasses. The words on the glass were illegible. They hadn't made sense before that anyway. He stepped closer to the windows to try to clear his vision. Instead he saw outside into the churchyard.

Things lurched toward the building. The purple, glowing rain both illuminated and distorted them. They looked neither human nor animal. Their hunched forms moved like slow cavemen except their nude bodies were devoid of hair. Their arms seemed extra long and discolored, even in the weird light.

David wanted to run back to his bedroom, hide under

the covers, and wake up from his dream, but the pulsing and humming from the pit seemed to push him closer to the window. He pressed his face against the glass and felt the raindrops roll down his cheeks as if he'd been pushed through the glass.

The creatures kept coming toward him. They just seemed to appear out of the rain. One popped up before his face. Its eyes bulged wetly out of its skull. The lips seemed overly full. It opened its mouth and croaked with the sound of a thousand toads.

David startled awake. He fell between the pew he lay on and the one in front of him. Morning light filtered through the windows. The brightness shocked him. The creatures and the purple rain were the last things he remembered.

A loud banging sounded on the door. He jumped up from the floor and hurried to open it. Thomas stood on the other side. His toad-like stature gave David another startle. It was like his nightmare stood before him.

"Mr. Marsh has sent for you," Thomas eyed him. "I'd suggest you not leave him waiting."

"Just let me get a sweater. Your town is awful damp," David said and realized that all his clothes were still in his car at Marsh's house. "Never mind; my stuff is there."

He followed the chauffeur and was whisked away to Marsh's old plantation home. Thomas drove a different route than the one that had brought David to the church. They passed by a small park that perched on what looked like a man-made terrace. A wrought-iron fence surrounded it. A statue holding a Civil War era rifle stood on top of a pedestal that looked like a high oak stump. A cannon sat before the statue. David couldn't get a good look at it, but it didn't look like the cannons he'd seen. He tapped on the window separating the two compartments. The driver pushed the window open but didn't say anything.

"What is that park back there?" David asked.

"Memorial," Thomas answered.

The car turned onto a familiar street. The downward sloping, oak-lined street led to the Marsh home. David saw the top of the house peeking over a magnolia.

"To what?" he asked.

"The battle."

Before he could ask what battle, Thomas closed the window and turned in to the short driveway that led to the back of the Marsh estate. David knew the driver was a man of few words, but he'd expected just a little more. He tapped on the glass again, but the driver stopped the car and got out. The door opposite him opened. David saw Marsh holding it open. He had a welcoming smile on his face.

"Good morning," Marsh said as David climbed out of the Lincoln.

"Good morning." David pressed on his hair, thinking that it must look mussed from being awakened right before leaving to come here.

"Did you sleep well?" Marsh closed the car door.

"Now that you mention it, not particularly. I had nightmares again and apparently some more sleepwalking. I woke up on a pew. I nearly broke my arm when Thomas's knocking startled me awake."

David walked toward the kitchen door. He intended to beat Marsh there and open it for his host. It would be the friendliest thing he could do. The other man took him by the arm and led him away from the house.

"I am sorry you have been having such fitful sleep. Perhaps you can tell me the nightmare as we stroll through my garden. I would like to hear about it. Maybe I could even shed some light on it," Marsh said.

"I don't know how. It was a bizarre one."

"I have some experience with dream interpretation. I've read all of Freud's work on the subject, even the obscure stuff that few people know about."

They walked down a brick sidewalk toward a stone wall. An arched gap allowed them into a flower garden. The sun peeked through the clouds. The light drew out the brilliant color from the plants growing along the side of the path. The spring had been good to Marsh's plants. Most of the flowers bloomed purple. A few red blossoms sprinkled diversity here and there. A whole patch of yellow flowers dazzled in the sun. David didn't recognize a single bloom, which he found odd because flowers had always been his wife's passion.

Marsh rested on a large wooden swing hanging from a low oak limb. He offered David the seat beside him. The wood and chain creaked as he sat down. It gave just a little with his weight. The swing began to sway back and forth as if blown by a breeze, but it was Marsh's movements that caused the action.

"I love sitting out here in the morning and at sundown," Marsh said. "The flowers make me feel young and vibrant."

"You're not old."

"Aren't I? I feel it. There is a great strain on the man responsible for an entire town. When my Louisa was alive, I shared some of the burden with her, but now I bear it alone."

"Are you the mayor too?"

Marsh shook his head. "We don't have any elected officials. You inherit the responsibility of running the town."

"Like a king? That doesn't seem very American."

"It's been our way since we settled in this country. The outside world doesn't care about what we do. We keep to ourselves and our ways. It is for the best." He waved toward the gate. Thomasine stood there holding a tray with a pitcher of tea on it. "Our refreshments. I know that you didn't enjoy your breakfast yesterday, so I opted to have Thomasine bring us some tea while we chat, and then prepare a midmorning lunch."

The maid stopped before them. Marsh took the pitcher and poured a glass. He gave it to David and then poured himself one. Thomasine walked away as David sipped his drink. The flavor of the tea popped in his mouth. He couldn't remember ever drinking such good sweet tea. A smile crossed his lips.

"I see that you enjoy this." Marsh tipped his glass, then drank.

"Very much. I was expecting unsweetened."

"Don't let that breakfast fool you. I am very much Southern. We're having good old-fashioned chicken and dumplings. Now, tell me about your dream."

David took another drink. He didn't want to relive the nightmare. It bothered him just thinking about it, but he replayed it for Marsh in its entirety, not leaving out a single thing. If his host could help him dispel some anxiety, he welcomed it.

Marsh nodded with interest as he listened. At times, he even smiled as if having a mini-epiphany. When David finished, he took a long drink from his tea.

"Dreams sometimes help us deal with stress," Marsh said. "According to Freud, they express our innermost secret desires. That is the reason your deceased wife appeared in the dream. You wish that she were with you to be a helpmeet. As you know, the Scriptures say God created woman for such a thing."

"I thought I was the preacher," David said.

"Yes, but I thought that needed to be mentioned." Marsh drank from his tea. "Dreams also can do something Freud never mentioned."

"What is that?"

"There are times and places where the veil between the living world and the world of the dead are thin and even torn. Sometimes dreams allow the two to cross over."

"I was dreaming about ghosts?" David almost laughed.

"Yes. There are things that you and I cannot completely understand. Ancient mysteries exist that even the greatest philosophical minds cannot grasp. Creatures exist that would madden most men if they knew about them."

"Ghosts seem a little extreme."

"What of your Holy Spirit?"

"Our Holy Spirit," David corrected. "That's a little different."

"What about the souls of men? Are those not energies absent of the body? Could they not manifest themselves? Physics explains that energy cannot be destroyed, only changed."

"But ghosts haunting my dreams? What about the light?"

"I told you that I would enlighten you on our faith and our history. Now is the time." Marsh eased back into the swing. It continued its slight sway. "This town was established well before Tennessee ever became a state. My ancestors were run out of the Massachusetts Bay Colony in the late 1600s. We roamed around looking for a place that we could be free from any restrictions of the government. We were led to this valley. The way in was arduous, which was perfect for our needs."

"Why were your ancestors driven from the colony?" David asked.

"Cotton Mather accused my ancestors of witchcraft. The church elders came to hang them all without trial. My ancestors slipped away in the night, risking Indian attack, but dying on their feet fighting was better than dying at the hands of zealots."

"Were they witches?"

"Of course not. They were accused of this because our religion was different from that of the Puritans. We worship things far more ancient than their books. Things before Adam and Eve."

"Do you mean Lilith?" David knew a little of the night demon from seminary. "No. She is just a myth. I mean things old and divine in their own ways."

David knew that God was older than Adam and Eve. Some people even worshipped angels. The Bible mentioned this. It didn't seem so extreme today, but he imagined that, in the uneducated times of Marsh's ancestors' migration, it would have been very odd.

"They built our town here. My house has been remade several times. The current look comes from times before the War. It took all we could do to keep our town from being reduced to ashes."

"What do you mean?" David asked.

"Just because we never owned slaves doesn't mean that the War didn't affect us. This town isn't far from Chattanooga. The Yankee soldiers came to our town and harassed us for a long time. One day we saw that they intended to attack. We had heard news from other parts of the state about looting and burning. Our town and its people had been persecuted enough. We took a stand."

"The town fought the Union army?"

"Not the whole thing, but a few platoons. We had enough guns to arm every man in town. We even had a cannon. It was mostly for celebratory activities and was very ornate, but it still fired."

"Is it in the memorial park?"

"Thomas brought you around that way just as I asked. How good of him. He isn't always the most obedient servant. The battle occurred all over the hills, but the fiercest of the action was located at the church. Many people lost their lives, but we beat the bluecoats back."

"How?"

"When your way of life is in danger, you will do anything. Our ancestors helped us as they still do today. That is why we have a homecoming every third Sunday of this month. That was the day of the battle and our victory."

"Do you think it is strange that I suggested having a decoration day on the exact same day?" David asked. That had been bothering him since yesterday.

"Not particularly. I probably mentioned something about it the night you arrived. I believe the dream you had last night was a memory of the battle. Great traumas leave scars not only on the skin but also on the energy of the world. I believe that our church is one of those places where the veil is very thin, if not torn. I also believe that one of the great ancient mysteries watches over the place."

"I would have never guessed the place had been the focal point of a battle. There isn't any sign. Is it the original building?"

Marsh nodded. "That is the building our forefathers built when they settled this valley. If you examine the exterior walls well, you will find pockmarks from bullets. I can even show you a hole in the wall surrounding the grounds caused by a cannonball."

"Amazing. There is so much history here. Maybe that is why I'm having the nightmares. Like you said, negative energy."

"I believe so." Marsh looked at his watch. "It is time to eat. Let's retire to the dining room."

There was just enough space in the bureau for David to fit his nice clothes inside. After lunch with Marsh, he'd spent the day putting away some of his personal belongings and making the apartment more livable. He wanted to avoid more nightmares, and brightening up the place might help him. Once everything was tidied up, he went for a walk in the churchyard. Some yellow wildflowers growing on the side of the hill opposite the backyard had caught his eye while he was unloading most of his car. They would definitely help liven up his cell, a little bit of the outdoors in the oppressively bleak room.

David tried to avoid thinking of his apartment as bleak, but the longer he stayed in there, the heavier and heavier it became. As he walked among the crooked headstones, he spied the flowers again. The round blooms stuck up from the dark grass like little balls of sunshine. The actual sun had disappeared into the clouds not long after he returned from Marsh's house. Now the sky darkened more because twilight neared. He walked to the back wall of the churchyard. An almost perfectly round hole hung midway up the wall. It had to be the cannonball hole Marsh spoke of.

David climbed onto the wall and jumped off on the back side. The ground sloped sharply upward. The damp grass and moss made climbing to the flowers difficult. After a few slips and slides, he picked a small bouquet of the wildflowers. They smelled as good as they looked. The musty aroma of his room would benefit from their perfume. He turned to head back to the wall. The first step sent his feet out from under him. David toppled down the hill. His head hit a rock outcropping. Everything went dark for a moment. He felt himself come to rest against the wall before his vision recovered.

As his vision regained full strength, he felt his head. A small amount of blood ran down his forehead from a cut. The bright, cheerful bouquet lay strewn down the hill. He wanted the flowers very much but didn't want to risk falling again and possibly killing himself. The wall seemed higher than before. He reached to pull himself over, but dizziness overcame him. Walking around the wall would be necessary.

He glanced through the hole in the wall to make sure the gate at the other side was open. It stood ajar. He had started to move around the wall when something in the church caught his eye. Purple light moved from window to window like someone carrying a candle. The slow ache rising in his head told him that he wasn't dreaming or in a delirium. Someone was there. He ran, despite the dizziness and aching head, to the gate. David leaned against it to steady himself.

The light still moved in the building. He steeled himself and charged to the church door. The small vestibule was dark. Only a faint glow of violet light could be seen. David stormed into the sanctuary. No one was there. The glow floated at the front of the room, over the pit. It looked like a flame. He ran down the aisle toward it. The flame pulsed brighter, then dimmer. He mounted the stage before the podium and reached out toward it. The flame snuffed out, leaving him standing in the dark. David fell to his knees and cried.

A thin twinge of pain creased David's face. He blinked awake and looked around the room through sleep-glazed vision. Ebenezer Hollingsworth closed a black leather bag. He took a wet rag and wiped it over David's head.

"You had a nasty fall," Ebenezer said. "What happened?"

David tried to prop up on his elbows. The other man pushed him back down and shook his head. The ceiling above him looked very familiar. He was back in the bedroom he'd been given at Marsh's house on the lumpy bed with the springs poking him in the exact same places as before.

"I don't know," David said. "How did I get here?"

"You drove yourself," Marsh said from behind him.

David tried to look back, but Ebenezer clucked his tongue at him. "Stay still. You probably have a concussion, and the last thing you need is to further agitate it."

"How did you hit your head?" Marsh walked into his line of vision. "All I know is that you banged on my door and pushed your way in. Blood streaked your face, and you ranted about a purple flame and wildflowers before you fainted."

Foggy memories floated in his head. He supposed it was the concussion. Images tumbled over themselves as he probed to remember. Feelings of fear and deep disappointment seemed to dominate his thoughts more than any particular image or memory.

"Are you a doctor?" he asked Ebenezer.

"Yes, but I would like to know how you hit your head."

David had asked the question to bide time until he found the proper memory. Both Marsh and Ebenezer stared at him. Their looks scrutinized his very soul. The look in their eyes seemed accusatory. No, that wasn't it; more like disappointment. For the life of him he couldn't figure out two things: exactly what had happened and why they would be disappointed by it.

"I can't remember."

The look of disappointment on Marsh's face grew deeper, but Ebenezer put his hand on David's shoulder.

"Can you remember anything? The smallest amount of information can be helpful."

"I remember joy, then worry. After that panic," David said.

"That doesn't help very much," Marsh said. "Those are just feelings. What happened?"

"Please, let me handle this, Alistair," Ebenezer waved his hand. "David, what made you feel that way? Something had to cause those emotions to be so strong that you remember them through your amnesiac state."

"I climbed the hill behind the church to pick wildflowers," David strained at his memory. It felt like a tight string being pulled in his mind. "I fell on my way back down because the slope was slippery."

"Can you not remember anything clearer than that?" Ebenezer asked. Irritability tinged his words.

David couldn't figure out why the doctor was so frustrated. He tried as hard as he could. The knock to his head obviously had addled his brain. Ebenezer needed to work on his bedside manner.

"Can I try something?" Marsh asked.

The question seemed to be directed to both of them. They said yes together. David really didn't know why he wanted to know what he couldn't remember. He needed the solace of knowing what caused such strong emotions.

Marsh reached into his pocket and brought out a marble. He blew on it and polished it on his sleeve. Another look satisfied him. He slid around so that David looked directly at him.

"I'm going to hypnotize you," he said. "Have you ever been hypnotized before?"

"No. I don't believe in that nonsense. It's just a bunch of hoodoo."

"Look into the glass ball," Marsh said. "What do you see?"

"A marble."

"Look beyond that, deep into the glass."

David stared at the small sphere. Smoky colors hung in the glass. They started to shift and move as he stared deeply into it. He felt his mind begin to loosen up as the rest of his body relaxed as if wrapped in the warmth of that smoke. He was flooded with memories. Not only did he remember how he hit his head, but he also remembered the painting of Marsh from the nightmare. The portrait gained new clarity. A whole army of the nightmare toad people stood behind Marsh. Fire burned behind that. The glow of it bordered the ridge. A ragged old American flag draped a body broken over the ornate cannon from the memorial park.

"Do you hear me?" Marsh asked from a thousand miles above David.

"Yes."

"What do you remember about hitting your head?"

"I fell because I slipped on the wet moss and hit my head on a rock. I saw the purple light like a candle glowing in the church. I rushed to find out who was carrying it around the sanctuary."

"Do you mean the purple light you have been seeing in your nightmares?"

"You are being flanked by an army of frogmen. A Union soldier is dead, draped in his flag. It's the painting from the third floor room where the purple glow came from," David said. "You look like you've never aged."

"What did you see when you went into the church after hitting your head?" Marsh redirected.

"A purple flame hung over that bottomless pit thing. It snuffed out."

Before Marsh could say anything else, the images before David's eyes changed. The smoke reappeared, but it pulsed with light, lavender light. It engulfed him. He struggled for breath as the light began to fill up his lungs and drown him.

"I'm drowning in the light. Help me," David yelled. "Anna, help me."

"He's seizing," Ebenezer said somewhere high above him. "Pull him back."

"Listen to my words, David," Marsh said. "Quit staring into the glass sphere. Let your mind surface and see me and Ebenezer."

"I can't. I'm drowning in the light."

An unseen hand slapped David on the cheek. The force of the blow ground his cheek into his teeth. The tinny taste of blood filled his mouth. The violet light dissipated, and he looked at Marsh and Ebenezer.

The doctor dug into his bag and brought out a small vial of liquid. He uncorked it and handed it to David. "Drink this."

"Why?"

"It will help you feel better. That elixir helps restore memory after a concussion."

"I didn't know there was a medicine for that." David looked at the dark red liquid.

"Not ordinary medicine, but I make some of my own. It will work. I guarantee it."

David didn't trust Ebenezer, but he didn't like the way he felt either. Everything swam around, and nothing seemed real. He swallowed the whole concoction. It tasted like red wine laced with berries. He didn't expect it to work.

"I am going to walk Ebenezer out, David," Marsh said, returning the marble to his pocket. "You will stay here tonight so that I can make sure you will be okay."

"I should really get back to the church. I need to work on my sermon."

"Nonsense. You need rest," Marsh said.

"He's right. Plus, you might have some complications from the concussion. There isn't a phone at the church, and you could need me," Ebenezer said. "The best thing is to rest."

"I've got a cell phone," David said.

"We get horrible signal here," Ebenezer answered

The two men walked out of the parlor. David settled back on the sofa. The room felt a bit stuffy. A wave of dizziness hit him when he stood to walk to the windows and open them for air. He staggered mid-room when he heard the two men talking on the other side of the door.

"Why do you think the light is affecting him so much?"

Ebenezer asked. "Do you think he might bolt before Sunday?"

"I don't. I believe the light affects him more because he is the real one. After so many years, I believe that we have found the *one*," Marsh said.

"I think he'll be crazy by Thursday evening."

"Why does that matter? He has talked about *God* giving him a calling to be here. The call is so strong that it has given him back some faith. He is the one; otherwise, the light wouldn't affect him this much. Most of the others have never even seen it."

"I hope so. I tire of this routine every year."

"I'm glad the other preacher canceled on us. I see wonderful things in our future." Marsh sounded pleased. "What did you give him?"

"A sleeping dram. It's so strong I don't think even the light will affect him." Ebenezer laughed.

David started to rush the door to accost the two men, but his head swam hard. A sudden attack of sleep overtook him. He had just enough time to sit on the couch before he fell dead asleep.

WEDNESDAY

David reached out and grabbed Thomasine by the arm as she tried to sneak from his room. She squealed and jerked away from him. His grip was too strong for her to wrench free.

"Let me go," she croaked.

"Why were you trying to sneak out?"

"Master Marsh said not to wake you. I was supposed to leave your breakfast on the nightstand and leave."

"Why is that?"

"He said because you needed your rest." Thomasine clammed up.

"Don't stop now; keep going."

"I've got nothing else to say."

David kept a secure hand on the maid and got out of bed. This entailed a degree of difficulty he hadn't expected, but he knew if he had let his grip slip just a little, Thomasine would have bolted for the door. The Marsh servants liked to dodge him and his questions at every opportunity. He pulled her with him to the door and closed it.

"Go sit on the sofa." He let go of Thomasine's arm.

She stood looking at him but didn't move. David pushed her toward the couch. Her feet scuttled across the floor. Again she made no effort to move by herself.

"Fine. If you want to stand, be stubborn," David said. He took a position between her and the door just in case she tried to make a dash for it. "You're still going to answer some questions for me.

"How did I end up in here? I passed out in the parlor."

"We brought you up here. Master Marsh believed you

would be more comfortable. I have work to attend to." She tried to walk past him.

"Not just yet." David blocked her. "Why did Ebenezer give me a sleeping potion?"

"I don't know."

"Why am I dreaming about purple lights?"

"I don't know."

"You don't know, or you won't tell: which is it?"

"She doesn't know," Marsh said from behind David.

He turned to see the master of the house wearing a smoking jacket and standing just inside the door. Thomasine pushed past David and left the room. Marsh shook his head.

"Have a seat," he pointed to the bed, "and eat your breakfast. You need food."

David sat down on the bed but left the tray of food on the table. "I'd rather not."

Marsh sat on the sofa and crossed his legs. "Why?"

"I don't know what's in it."

"I believe it's grits and melba toast."

"That's not what I mean, and you know it. I overheard you and Ebenezer talking last night. He gave me a sleeping potion."

"That is true."

"How do I know you've not drugged the food?"

"You don't, but why would I do that?"

"Why would you give me a sleeping potion?"

Marsh smiled a wry smile. "Because you needed to sleep. Ebenezer said the only way to help your brain heal was sleep."

"That's not right. You're not supposed to sleep if you have a concussion," David said.

"You're being irrational, Reverend Stanley. He's a doctor and knows more than both of us in this matter."

"What about all that talk about the nightmare light?"

"Have you or haven't you been having nightmares involving a pulsing purple light?" Marsh asked.

"Yes."

"We were talking about the nightmares. Ebenezer knew that his sleeping medicine would keep you from having those dreams. Sleep is the most important thing you can get. Without it, you'll go crazy."

David thought for a moment. He rolled the conversation he had overheard in his mind. Marsh did an excellent job explaining it. He hated it when he felt so silly. Everything had been a misunderstanding.

"I'm sorry," he said. "I guess I've just gotten rattled by the fall and the nightmares."

"It is understandable." Marsh stood. "Have your breakfast, and then you can go back to the church and work on your sermon."

"I'd really like to use the Internet. Do you have it here at the house?" David took the tray from the table and placed it on his lap.

"The Internet? No," Marsh answered.

"How about the library?" he asked through a mouth of grits. "Nothing in Innsboro has it. We are very far out."

"Not even dial-up?"

Marsh walked to the door. "Our phone lines are very poor. They've not been updated in many years."

David bit a piece of melba toast. "I guess I'll have to use my cell phone when I get back to the church. It's slow going, and I don't know how much time I have left on my plan."

"Cell phone signal is atrocious here as well, like Ebenezer said last night. They are practically useless. You can leave when you get ready. I will give you my good-byes now. I have work to do in town and probably won't be here when you depart."

"Thank you for everything," David said.

Marsh gave a small bow and left. David finished his breakfast and set the tray back on the table. Rain spattered against the window. It seemed it rained every day in this town. He walked to the window and looked out. His room faced the street. Marsh's Lincoln drove down the street toward the town. David decided to go back to the church and get some work done.

Trepidation filled David as he looked at the doors to the church. He wanted to get back in his car and drive away. At the same time, God tugged at his heartstrings. A voice told him that these townspeople needed saving. David agreed. Something about the town and the people felt strange, like a group of people doomed forever. He didn't like that feeling. If being their preacher might save them from eternal damnation, he would do it. David stormed into the church.

Despite the gloominess outside, the sanctuary seemed brighter than it had. A lemony odor hung in the air. Everything smelled fresh. He walked to the windows. The dust that had streaked them just the day before was gone. The cemetery beyond the wall looked as clear as if he stood in it. He absentmindedly put his hand on the curved back of a pew. The wood felt slick as if oiled. The smell of melting paraffin wax with the fragrance of lemons wafted over him. He looked at the ceiling. Light flickered from the chandelier. Long taper candles melted halfway down. The church had been cleaned. It looked amazing.

"Hello?" he said loudly into the room.

"What?" a voice croaked from behind the pulpit.

"Who's there?" David asked.

A pudgy woman with her gray hair pulled back under a black scarf toddled up the steps to the podium platform. She wore a maid's black uniform with a white apron. A wooden bucket hung from one hand, and the other clutched a scrub brush.

"Who are you?" she asked.

"I'm Reverend David Stanley."

She smiled. It was unpleasant, showing far too many teeth and too much gum. When the skin on her face wrinkled, all her features disappeared. Her face looked like a piece of chewed gum.

"Very happy to meet you. I'm Hester. Mr. Fernwell sent me to clean the church for Sunday. It's our big day. He wanted it spic-and-span."

"Mr. Fernwell?" David searched his memory of the last few days. His brains still seemed a bit addled from the fall.

"Nahum Fernwell. He's one of the elders," Hester said.

"I remember. Please excuse me. I had a fall yesterday and have a slight concussion, according to the doctor."

"Doctor?"

"Ebenezer Hollingsworth."

Hester blew a raspberry. "I'm more of a doctor than he is."

"You're a little different from the other servants I've met," David said.

"I ain't a servant. Well, not anymore. My master's family has been dead for years. I guess being without one that long makes my tongue a little looser."

"Do they prevent you from talking?" David said. "The master's family."

"They discourage it," Hester said.

David took a moment to consider things. Perhaps this cleaning lady could answer questions for him.

"Do you know anything about an eerie purple light that might float round in here?"

"Yep."

"Can you tell me about it?"

Hester shook her head.

"Nope."

"Why not?"

"Ain't proper to talk about things I've never seen."

"But you know a legend or something about it. You can tell me that."

She shrugged. "Ain't anything to tell. I reckon it's like the will–o'–the–wisp or foxfire. Preacher, unless you need me for anything else, I'm done here."

"That's fine." He looked up at the candles. "How do I put those out?" He pointed.

"Let them burn out. Won't cause any issues."

Hester plodded past him and out of the church. As he stared at the candles flickering close to the ceiling, David decided he should give her a ride home. When he went to the door, she was gone. He walked to his car and looked both ways down the road. A light mist floated around but didn't interfere with visibility much. The maid wasn't anywhere to be seen.

"Will-o'-the-wisp," he said aloud.

He'd heard about that but didn't really know what it was. His grandfather called it foxfire and said it showed up out over the swamps where he grew up, but David had never seen it.

It had never been described as purple that he could remember. Maybe his phone would get enough signal for him to consult Google.

His apartment felt like a tomb after coming through the clean-smelling sanctuary. The air smelled musty and stale. Even opening the window didn't help. The damp outside air only brought in the heady smell of rot and wet pine needles. It didn't sit well on his stomach, leaving him queasy.

David grabbed his phone and headed back to the sanctuary. As he crossed over into the church, he saw that his phone had no signal. He stepped on the podium platform, but the signal bar remained the same. Marsh had not been lying. The phone didn't even give a hint that it would find signal. Maybe he needed to get higher, out of the small valley.

David left the church building. He walked across the cemetery to his car. Nothing came up or down the road, so pulling out was simple. He eased the car up the road toward the main highway. The shoulder on his side of the road was narrow, and a deep ditch dropped off from there. The other side plummeted to the hollows and valley below. David carefully watched both his phone and the road. The last thing he needed was to meet another tanker truck barreling down the mountain and end up turtled at the bottom of a hollow.

Driving higher up the mountain had no impact on the signal. The phone showed no signal bars. He shook the phone as if that would help, but still no change.

"Come on," he shouted. "There is no way there is this big of a dead zone."

David stared at his phone, willing it to get a signal. He looked back to the road and saw several boulders blocking his way. The excessive rain likely had caused the rockslide. He slammed on the brakes. The car fishtailed as the tires squealed on the pavement. David braced himself, ready to topple down the side of the mountain. Instead, the car spun and slammed into the rocks. The passenger side crumpled in toward him. The impact jarred his phone out of his hand. It clattered to the passenger-side floorboard. The car stopped. He looked out the windshield. Through spiderweb cracks, the great drop-off stared back at him.

With a clarity that only a near-death experience can bring, David looked around. Adrenaline amplified his senses. The car idled. Nothing knocked in the engine, which was a good thing. He shifted the gears to park and reached to the floorboard for his phone.

David eased the car into reverse. Metal ground as the car moved against the rocks. When he was sure he could turn without dropping a tire off the side of the road, he put the car in gear and started toward the church. Everything seemed okay. The tires didn't blow out as he slowly descended the mountain. His brakes held out. The whole way back he kept staring at his phone, hoping for some signal. Now he wanted just enough signal to make a call to the outside world and let someone know where he was. For some reason, despite what God was telling him, the idea of being trapped in Innsboro scared him. No signal appeared.

As he neared the church, rain began to splatter the windshield. He looked up to turn on the wiper blades and hoped they'd work across the broken windshield. Glowing purple water hit the windshield instead of rain. The entire windshield became a flashing neon sign. David screamed and slammed the brakes. The car pulled to the passenger side, threatening to skid off the road.

The wipers swiped the water from the windshield. The glow turned into a fog. The engine shut off. The car sat dead on the side of the road. The violet fog began to sift into the cabin. David still depressed the brake. He shifted the gears to neutral and let off the brake. The car rolled downhill. Without power, the brakes wouldn't be much good, but anything was better than being eaten by the purple light. The car rolled faster. He sailed past the church, taking the curve toward town so fast the tires squealed. The road flattened out, and the car coasted down Main Street and slowed as the slope of the street leveled off. He stood on the brakes. The car stopped. He looked at his phone, hoping that he might finally, just by luck, have signal so he could call 911. The phone was dead.

David tried to turn the engine over. It wouldn't make a noise. He knew the cause. The battery was drained. The same thing must have happened to his cell phone. The purple light had absorbed the energy. Something strange was going on. He was going to find out what.

No cars moved down the street. The whole town looked as uninhabited as it had on the Sunday he found the place. David walked toward the hub of town. He saw the old gas station on the other side of the creek. No cars sat at the pumps, but the tanker he'd passed on Sunday sat beside the building. The wind began to blow. The air felt chilly and damp. Not surprising since a fine mist still floated in the air.

David turned to look back up the mountain road. He expected to see the light following him. Instead, the slick black ribbon disappeared around a curve. His broken-down car looked at him from the shoulder. Despair began to fill him up. Only his car gave him any real independence he could have in the town. Without it, David knew that he was at the will of Alistair Marsh and the other elders. He had been beginning to trust Marsh until he met Hester. She changed his mind. Her candor made him think things were being hidden from him.

The old woman must have been faster than he thought she could be. He hadn't spotted her on the road as he barreled back down the mountain. Perhaps she'd fallen off into the ravine. Something more sinister came to David's mind. Marsh might have eliminated her. For some reason, David felt Marsh and the elders were capable of such things.

His ponderings bounced around in his mind, sending his thoughts down one tangent after the other until he was lost in a tangle of speculation and conjecture as harrowing as the forested mountains that surrounded Innsboro. He was so lost in these thoughts that he didn't notice walking through town and into the library. The dusty smell of old books snapped him back to the present. He looked around the room. His intent had been to find the town library, if it had one. It seemed that his feet brought him there on autopilot.

A small circulation desk took up the space in the middle of the floor. The walls were lined with bookshelves. The only space between the shelves was for the windows, which seemed to provide the ambient light in the room. A few tables with chairs littered the floor. Lamps with green glass shades sat on the tables to provide further light. David stepped deeper inside. No librarian greeted him. The whole place seemed as though no one had been there in a while. He ran his finger through a thin layer of dust on the circulation desk.

"Hello," David yelled.

His call echoed off the walls. Nothing moved in the place. He needed help to find exactly what he sought. A map or atlas might be the best place to start. If he could find another way out of town, he might be able to access the Internet.

David wandered around the main room until he found the card catalog. In most libraries he had been to lately, a computer database made this piece of furniture obsolete. He hadn't seen a single computer in the place, not even an antiquated one. For that matter, the library appeared devoid of any modern machines. The place felt stuck in some other time.

That was it. The idea popped in his head like a lightbulb burning out. The whole town seemed trapped in a time warp. Marsh's old Lincoln and the absence of modern necessities or the Internet or cell phones testified to this. Now that he gave his attention to the thought, even people's clothes were outdated. They didn't wear leisure suits or frilly cravats, but the clothes had a thrift-store quality to them.

He slid the "A" drawer out before remembering that an atlas would be in the reference section. Large signage was a convenient feature of the Innsboro Public Library. He easily found the reference section and a US atlas. David took the book back to one of the tables, opening it to Tennessee as he did.

The lettering on the map was small, but with the additional light from a lamp, David found the highway he'd traveled before turning off on the road to town. He traced the line up from Chattanooga, looking for the cutoff road to the town as he did. His finger crossed the border into North Carolina. The road to town never appeared. He flipped to the town index in the back. Tennessee listed no town named Innsboro. David looked at the date of the atlas. The year 2000 stared up at him in bold, square letters. The atlas was old, but the town was older.

"What are you doing here?" Marsh asked, pushing a cart

loaded with books from another room.

David jumped up from the table, slamming the atlas closed. "I was looking up roads out of town."

"Why would you do that?"

"I tried to get up to the main highway so that I could get a cell phone signal, but a rockslide blocked the road. I figured there has to be another way out of town."

"There isn't," Marsh said.

"So we're trapped?"

"We are all trapped in our own way," Marsh said. "It is nothing to get excited about."

"What if we have a medical emergency of some kind?"

"Ebenezer Hollingsworth can handle anything we need. He is a very good doctor." Marsh pushed the cart past David.

He grabbed hold of the cart to stop it. "That's not what I've heard. I was told he isn't even a doctor."

Marsh chuckled. "That's crazy. Who told you that?"

"Hester, the lady who cleans the church."

"Hester?" The other man thought for a long time. "We don't have a Hester in this town."

"You have to. I saw her with my own eyes. We talked. She said that Mr. Fernwell sent her to clean."

"Do you mean the Gilmans' servants?" Marsh asked.

"She said her master's family was dead, so I don't know." David took a book from the cart.

"That's her. The Gilmans have been gone a long time. I would have thought she'd moved on." Marsh said the last part dreamily. "I can't imagine why a servant would stay without a family."

"So you have people leave Innsboro?"

"Eventually."

"How can they do that? According to that atlas, the town doesn't exist." David poked the atlas with the book he had in his hand.

"Please be careful with that book. We only have so many children's books. We must take good care of them."

David turned the book over in his hands. A picture of the Br'er Rabbit and the Tar-Baby looked up at him from the glossy board cover. The book looked very old, but in remarkably good shape. He opened it to the copyright page. It read 1924.

"This book is in great shape for its age," he said.

"We try to keep it that way. Books are hard to come by." Marsh took it back. "Children's books especially."

"So you have children in the town?"

"Of course we do; what kind of town doesn't have children?"

"I've not seen a school, a playground or any evidence of children," David said. "I've never been to a town with children that didn't have those things."

Marsh put the book back on his cart. "I'm going to guess that until today you didn't know that we had a library either. Reverend, there are many things about us that you don't know. There are many things that you assume, and I am afraid that they are all bad or conspiratorial."

"You keep a lot of mystery around yourself."

Marsh moved to the table. He opened the atlas to Tennessee. After studying the map for a moment, he poked his finger at an empty stretch of land north of Chattanooga and east of the North Carolina border.

"That's us," he said.

David looked. Not a single road led off the main highway to his finger. Only the blue line of a creek scarred the green picture. He got closer so he could read the name of the creek. There wasn't one.

"Why isn't the town on the map?" he asked.

"Because we aren't welcomed anywhere, even though we settled the area before anyone else. I told you about our ancestors leaving Massachusetts because of Cotton Mather. Tennessee tried to move us, but because we defeated the Union in a battle, they didn't feel they could, so they marked us off the map. Plain and simple."

"Do you still pay taxes?" David didn't know why he asked this. It just came out.

"Yes. We do everything any citizen would. We are just not acknowledged. As far as Hester is concerned, don't listen to her. A servant without a family is given to strange delusions."

"Okay, but what about the rockslide?"

"I'll let the others know when my duties as librarian end. We take it time about, you see. I think you should go back to the church and study," Marsh said.

"I can't. My car is shot."

"What happened?"

"I skidded on the wet road and hit the rocks at the landslide. Then when I turned around to come into town to let someone know, I passed through a purple fog like I've been dreaming about. It fried all the electronics in the car, including my cell phone."

Marsh looked worried. "That cannot be. You've only dreamed about that light. Surely it was your concussion causing you to see things."

"My car is on the side of the road just outside of town, banged up and dead as a doornail."

"I can give you a ride back to the church. You can study here in the meantime. The Bibles are over there." He pointed to a shelf on the opposite wall.

"I think I'll look up will-o'-the-wisp," David said.

"Whatever for?"

"Hester said the purple light was like that."

"The will-o'-the-wisp is caused by swamp gas," Marsh said. "I don't think swamp gas is causing your nightmares."

David nodded and agreed that swamp gas wasn't doing that. However, the light he'd just experienced wasn't a dream or a hallucination. Something strange lived in Innsboro, and it wasn't just the citizens.

THURSDAY

David ate breakfast at the small table in his apartment. It was leftover dinner. Marsh had taken him home for dinner and packed up some for him to eat at breakfast, with the promise of sending Thomas out to take him to the market so he could fix his own meals and not have to depend on Marsh's hospitality.

Ham made a good breakfast food, but the instant mashed potatoes, which had been dry and lacking any hint of butter at dinner, were hard to swallow that morning. Water to wash everything down didn't help either. He was certain by the almost artificial flavor of the meat that the ham was canned.

After eating all the ham and only a small bit of the potatoes, David pushed the plate away. Last night had passed without a single dream or any sleepwalking. For some reason, he'd decided to try an experiment. A box in the corner of his apartment contained religious gifts that congregation members had given him through the years. Most of them took a Catholic bend. A few statues of the Virgin Mary in sacred blue, Jesus holding the thorn-latticed heart, and a gaudy crucifix made up part of the collection. David had never gotten rid of them because in some ways he liked iconography. He took a few of the items and placed them around the apartment. A gold cross on a chain still hung from his neck as he decided to get dressed and wait for Thomas in the cemetery. The icons must have kept the nightmares and the light away.

David had never thought of dreams as supernatural. He'd read Freud's treatise on them just like Marsh claimed to have done. His introductory psychology professor had given him an excellent grade on an essay about dreams many years ago.

Everything he believed about the nature of them had changed when he woke up in Marsh's third-floor hall after looking through a dream keyhole. He kept the cross hanging around his neck as he buttoned a French blue shirt. The symbol would remain hidden. Marsh and the other elders might not like him openly wearing a cross. Exploration of the church had come up empty on any Christian imagery except that strange star. He wanted to check the headstones in the graveyard to see if they bore any such imagery. He decided to do it while waiting for his ride. It gave him just enough time to look at a few markers.

David looked at the yellow legal pad lying on his unmade bed. Cursive writing in thick, black ink covered about half of the page. He had worked since Monday and all that had come was half a page of notes. Never had a sermon been so hard to write. He began to think that the church itself hindered him from working. If the library felt cozier, he'd moved his work there, but it felt more claustrophobic than his small apartment.

The air felt chilly when David stepped out of the church door. The clouds hung so low, he thought if he stood on tiptoe and stretched his arm as far as he could, his fingers would brush through them. Maybe it was high fog instead of low clouds. Morning dew pooled on the grass in the cemetery. The old headstones glistened with it as well. The whole world seemed covered in a film of water this morning. David stepped off the sidewalk into the grass. The cuffs of his pants became wet. No one would care, he suspected.

The first stone he came to tilted to the left. The etching on its face had faded away into history. He knelt and ran his finger over the indention where the lettering was. His digit read what his eyes couldn't, as if he were reading braille. A woman named Dorcas, no last name, lay beneath that grave marker. David figured she must have been one of the servants. As of yet, he'd not heard nor been told the last name of any of the servants. Marsh only called his servants Thomas and Thomasine. Hester had never mentioned her last name. He remembered an old house in Alabama he'd been to once. A family burial plot occupied part of that abandoned property. Most the headstones bore the names of different family

members, except for one. It read *Tobias*. The family's most
loyal slave had received that marker of his final resting place
without a last name.

Marsh said that the town had not owned slaves because
of its servant class, but it now seemed that the servants were
slaves that just hadn't come from Africa. He walked toward
some of the stones butting against the church foundations. The
lettering on these stones had passed the test of time better. A
simple stone, rounded at the top like a stereotypical tombstone,
read *Nahum Fernwell, b. 1800*. No death date was present. David
stared at this for a little while. He had met Nahum Fernwell,
but it wasn't possible for him to be the one supposedly buried
there. The next stone in line bore the name E. Hollingsworth
and a date of 1815. This headstone didn't look two hundred
years old. Instead, it might have been there for about forty
years. Beside this a monument with a decorative design like
an all-seeing eye bore the name Ernest Greenbough with the
date of 1785 only. Just to side of this ancient fellow, David read
a stone that said "Gregor Armstrong 1768, ascended a new
plane". He thought back to the day he met the elders and they
talked of their ancestors being in this place. It seemed that
they might have a different view of death, not as an end but
as something where they lived on. It was Christian idea, but
he'd found that few Christians actually thought like that. Their
ideas of death felt refreshing to him. He thought that he might
like preaching in this town despite some of the doubts he had.

A car horn blew. It echoed off the limestone of the
mountain and the hewn stones that formed the church. He
jumped around to see Marsh's Lincoln idling at the entrance
gate. Thomas sat behind the wheel, looking straight at him.
The horn echoed out again. David waved his hand toward the
chauffeur and made his way across the graveyard, careful not
to trip over any of the stones.

The car felt pleasant when David sat in the backseat. The
window between the front and back was open to let the air
conditioner blow its cool air to him. For the first time that
morning, he didn't feel like he was trapped in a grave with
hundreds of pounds of dirt bearing down on him.

"I'm supposed to take you to the market," Thomas said in flat tones.

"Yes. I'm sorry to have to bother you with it, but my car broke down."

"Master Marsh told me about it. I towed it to the filling station. I ought to be fixing it instead of this. You could do your own shopping." Thomas turned the car onto the road heading toward town.

"Again, I'm sorry. I didn't want to inconvenience you."

"Nothing but inconvenience my whole life."

David leaned toward the window. "Don't you like your job?"

"I've done the same thing for a hundred years. Always the same, no different."

"I guess if you are stuck in a rut, it might seem like a hundred years or a million," he said. "I know that's how my job felt after my wife died. Now I've found this place, and it's given me hope."

"Scared you too, I'd bet," Thomas drove past the library toward a part of the town David hadn't been to.

"I won't disagree with that." He leaned back afraid Thomas might slam on the brakes and his face against the glass. "You seem awful defiant this morning."

"Why not? Sunday, Decoration Day, is almost here. Nothing's going to change, and it'll be another year until we have another one."

"I didn't realize that Sunday was so important to the people of the town. You hold your history very highly."

Thomas huffed what sounded like a sarcastic laugh. "History, indeed."

The car pulled into the parking lot of a very old-looking supermarket. The other spaces were empty. David leaned down to peer out of the windshield. No one appeared to be milling around in the store either.

"Not a very popular place? I guess once people realize the road is blocked, they'll empty it out."

"Everyone already has what they need. They get it when the truck first comes in. No one wants last year's products," Thomas said. "Can you get out without me opening the door for you?"

"Of course." David did so. He walked toward the entrance but stopped by the driver's-side window. Thomas rolled it down. "Do you have a last name?"

"Marsh."

"You and Alistair are kin?"

"All servants have their master's last name, unless their masters are dead. Then they have no last name," Thomas said.

David nodded and headed into the grocery store. The usual smell of baked goods and produce didn't hit him when he stepped inside. Instead the air smelled stale and slightly metallic. He glanced around. There were only seven aisles. No freezers or coolers lined the walls. Neither bins of fresh produce nor racks of bread were in evidence. A frail woman in clothes sized for a woman much larger than herself stood behind an old-fashioned cash register. Her skin almost looked like it was falling off the bones. It was as if she had been a rotund woman and suddenly had all the fat under her skin removed.

"Where is the bread?" David asked.

"Don't have any. Canned goods only."

"No milk?"

"Powdered or evaporated only."

"Is there another market in town?" He thought anything would be better than this place.

"This is it, like it or lump it. Ain't much of anything you'd probably want anyway. Most of the good stuff's been bought up. Reckon you can pick over and see what will suit you."

David took a hand basket and walked down the first aisle. Canned black beans and field peas lined the shelves. The labels only had the picture of the food and black-and-white words identifying the product. No brand name dazzled him. He went down the next aisle and found canned fruit, but not peaches or pears. Plums and currants lined the shelves. He found the jars of preserves, but again, they were made from fruits most Americans didn't eat.

He started collecting cans of the least offensive foods. On the meat aisle he lucked out and found generic Spam and Vienna sausages. He liked both of those. Despite no fresh loaves of bread, the place had lots of saltine crackers. Meals might be like those eaten while camping, but it would suffice until the road to the highway was cleared and he could find a Walmart, Winn-Dixie or even a Piggly Wiggly.

The checkout counter was just that, a counter. No conveyer belt ran the goods closer to the clerk, and certainly no barcode scanner rested in the middle. The old lady punched the price into the ancient cash register. She shoved each item into a brown paper sack she'd opened beside her. No care was given to the order of the sacked items. David felt lucky that the store didn't have bread or eggs because they would have been demolished by her carelessness.

"Why isn't there any bread or fresh meat?" David asked as the woman punched in the price for the crackers.

"Can't eat it fast enough," she said, cramming the crackers into the bag.

"What does that mean?"

The last item was a can of mushrooms. She slammed her fingers on the register tabs.

It sounded like bone hitting bone.

"We can't get it all eaten by Decoration Day. Distributor won't give us a small enough supply. They say it ain't profitable." The total rang up. "Your total is $24.50, correct change only please, no checks, and certainly no credit cards, so don't even ask."

David dug a $20 and $5 bill from his billfold. He gave it to the clerk. "Keep the change."

"I was going to anyway." She heaved the sack of groceries onto the counter and flopped the ribbon of receipt in with the purchases. "Have a good day, preacher."

David took the heavy sack of cans and left the grocery store. He opened the door with his hip and hoped he didn't drop the sack on his foot. With the road still blocked, a broken foot might be something that the *local* doctor couldn't handle. Thomas opened the car door for him when he approached. He placed the sack on the bench seat and shoved it across as he crawled in. The chauffeur closed the door just as if David were his master. A thought struck him when he saw the old checkout woman step out of the store onto the sidewalk—she'd called him preacher. He wondered how she knew that. As far as David knew, neither

Marsh nor any of the other elders had announced his arrival. She looked like one of the servant class with less fat, so she might have heard it word of mouth. Innsboro was the smallest town he'd ever found himself in.

"Thomas, how did the checkout lady know that I was the new preacher? Has Mr. Marsh made an announcement?"

"Doesn't have to. Word travels fast."

That affirmed what David thought. He reached into his sack and took out a can of Vienna sausage. It had been a long time since he'd had them: probably the last time he'd gone fishing, which had to be nearly ten years. A juicy steak would be better than anything he had in his sack. Even scrambled eggs could beat oversalted canned meat. At least they had Spam and not sardines. If all he'd had to eat were sardines, weight loss would be no problem. Marsh had served kipper the first morning David had come to town. Nothing at any of the meals he'd eaten with the man had been fresh. The vegetables were canned, the mashed potatoes instant, and the ham had been Dak or the black-and-white-labeled equivalent, no doubt.

"Why is there no fresh food in the market?" he asked Thomas.

"There's not enough time to eat it all," the driver answered.

"That's what the clerk said, but it doesn't make sense. Why can't you finish it?"

"Not enough time before Decoration Day," Thomas said.

David rubbed his temples. The circular thinking of these people gave him a headache. "But why does that matter?"

"We can't eat it after Decoration Day," Thomas said as if this were completely logical and he'd never thought it a strange thing.

"You can't eat fresh food after Decoration Day?"

Thomas reached behind him and closed the window between the front and rear seats. David tapped on the glass, but the driver ignored him. The preacher leaned back and decided to enjoy the ride to the church. Once Thomas decided to clam up, he wouldn't be able to pry a word out of him with a crowbar. Never had he encountered such stubborn people. At least none of the town officials need worry about loose lips sinking ships in Innsboro.

The ride was short, sweet, and silent. Thomas remained in

the car, forcing David to get out and close the car door without dropping the heavy sack of groceries. The walk down the small steps to his apartment proved a challenge as well, mostly because David kept looking over his shoulder for the purple glow. The rain started again as he put his canned goods away.

The idea of no one eating fresh food after Sunday worried him. Nothing logical could explain this behavior. The only thing close was the idea that perhaps the town was abandoned after Decoration Day and reinhabited shortly before. It would explain why the previous preacher only gave one sermon and supposedly stole the refrigerator. David hoped that wasn't the case. He hated the idea of having a new preaching job for only one day. God had told him to come to that place and revived his faith just for that purpose. The feeling of revival filled him to the brim. Inspiration whispered in his ear. He knew how to continue his sermon but could not work in that cell. God told him to go to the cemetery and write. The air would do wonders for his abilities. If it still rained, God said the better to wash away the bad ideas.

David grabbed the legal pad from the bed and a pen from the table. He didn't need his Bible because God was going to tell him what to write. The air outside felt cooler, and the rain had stopped. The grass in the cemetery remained wet. He sat in an open spot despite this. The water began to soak his backside. David wrote.

It took only a few minutes for his divine inspiration to finish the first page of the legal pad and move him to the second. The words flowed like nothing he had ever experienced in his time as a minister. Everything came to a crashing halt when a burst of purple light in his side vision grabbed his attention.

David looked in the direction of the light. Instead of the nightmare glow, a woman stood over a headstone. He had no idea how she had slipped past him into the cemetery. The patch of ground he sat on was near the gate.

The woman wore black with a veil over her face. A white handkerchief clasped in her hand trembled as if in a breeze, but the air was still. The woman cried. David stood, brushed off the back of his pants, and let the legal pad fall to the wet grass along with his pen.

"Are you okay, miss?" he asked.

The woman looked toward him, then back down at the headstone. David took a step toward her. As he watched, she evaporated into violet mist. He rubbed his eyes and blinked as hard as he could. Nothing of the woman remained.

David began to think that he was hallucinating. The stress of everything had to be getting to him. To indulge his curiosity, he walked to the headstone. It looked as old as many of the others, but the letters etched into the rock had held up better than most. He recognized the name, but the date bothered him. It read *Louisa Marsh, 1832–1864, Beloved wife and mother.* David glanced at the smaller stone beside Louisa's grave marker. The fading words said *Henry Marsh, 1856–1864.*

He looked up at the church. Once again, the purple flame moved around the sanctuary past the windows. Someone definitely carried it this time. The woman in black who had disappeared at the grave moved back and forth, waving the hideous light as if to tempt David back into the building.

The preacher ran inside, trampling his sermon underfoot as he passed. The woman carried an invisible candle topped by the purple flame.

"What is this?" he yelled at her.

She came toward him, bearing the candle ahead. The black veil obscured her face, and she said nothing.

"In the name of all that is holy in this house of God, what are you?" David yelled.

The flame flickered out, but the woman kept coming closer. He could almost touch her. When she drew close enough, David grabbed hold of her veil and pulled it down. The fabric slipped away from her face.

Instead of a human visage or even a skull, a horrible mass of entwined, squirming, tentacle-like projections reached out from where the face should have been. They groped for him. He let go of the veil and stumbled backward. Terror like he never felt before engulfed him. His feet slipped on the hardwood floor, and he toppled, hitting his head on the edge of a pew. His world didn't go dark, but lilac.

FRIDAY

Through the filmy vision of roused sleep, David saw a lavender glow at the edges of the ceiling. He blinked hard to clear his sight, but everything remained veiled and gossamer. The room wasn't his apartment. The purple glow revealed enough of the ceiling for him to know that he wasn't lying on the floor of the church sanctuary either. He stared at the ceiling in Marsh's guest room.

David sat up in bed. The springs creaked and poked into his bottom. In the brief time he'd drunk, no hangover had been this bad. The nightmare glow didn't bother him. He needed to know how he had ended up in Marsh's house. The last thing he remembered was the woman in black with the tentacles coming out from her face.

The glow began to thrum. The feeling of it throbbed through his head. It rattled his teeth. The light demanded his attention. Never had it been this intense.

"What do you want?" he said aloud, looking up at the ceiling and holding his hands over his temples.

The light pulsed and thrummed harder. The rhythm of it took on the quality of language. The light tried to communicate with him, but he had no idea what it said.

"I don't understand you."

"Come to me," the light said in David's head. The words matched the cadence of the pulsing.

"Who are you? Are you God?" he whispered, afraid to speak too loudly to the Almighty.

"Come to me."

David didn't waste time. He felt the light inside like the

warmth God had sent to revive his faith. The rhythmic pulsing of the light fell into the same pattern as his steps as he walked out of his room and into the corridor. The whole hallway ceiling glowed. The light dipped like dripping water. He stretched his hands up at the drooping light as he walked toward the stairs. His fingers brushed over the energy. His arm hair stood on end like he was too close to an electrical field. The light drooped even lower, but not around his hands. The lights in the hall blinked out just like his phone and car had when he'd driven through the purple fog.

At the foot of the steps, David looked up. The light spilled out from the third floor. Excitement almost overwhelmed him. The light had been such a burden when he thought of it as a nightmare. Now that it was God, it excited him more than anything else ever had. Soon he would be in direct contact with the Almighty. Any doubt he'd had about staying in Innsboro left him.

As he started up the first step, a hand touched him on the shoulder. A surge of excitement jolted through him. God touched him, but none of the electrical feeling of the light joined the touch.

"Where are you going?" Marsh asked.

David looked down at the man. Grave concern etched lines on Marsh's face. The preacher tried to brush the other man's hand off his shoulder.

"I'm going to the light, to God."

"There is no light," Marsh said.

David looked at the third floor. The light still spilled over the edge of the landing, but had dwindled. He reached toward it.

"It's boiling out like fog," he said.

"There is nothing there. Let me take you back to your room. You don't need to be out of bed. Ebenezer said that your fall has aggravated the concussion. You're probably hallucinating," Marsh stepped around him and tugged on him to go back to his room.

"What is the problem?" Ebenezer asked, coming up the stairs.

"Reverend Stanley has wandered out of his room, trying to get to the light that he's been dreaming about," Marsh said.

"It is real. I see it spilling from the third floor." David pointed down the hallway, which was now lit with electric light. The God light no longer drooped down but clung to the flat ceiling.

"You need to return to your room," Ebenezer said. "Alistair found you unconscious on the floor of the church. You've aggravated the concussion you received. You need to get off your feet."

"The light is God. He wants me to come to him," David almost raved.

"He is hallucinating," Ebenezer said to Marsh. "Get the others up here to help get him to his room. I'll go get some medication to help him."

"Nahum, Horace, please help me," Marsh yelled down to the ground floor.

Ebenezer let go of David's arm, but before he attempted to wrench himself away from Marsh, the other men were upon him. They dragged him down the hallway and back into his room. Without any ceremony, they flung him onto the bed. The springs sank and jabbed into his back. The men loomed over him, holding him place. David thought about lashing out, but they kept a secure grip while pressing him down.

"Don't you understand that the light is God?" He looked up at the ceiling. The purple light continued to shine around the edges of the moldings. "He called to me."

"He took quite a bump to the head," Marsh told the others. "He believes the light from his nightmares is talking to him. Ebenezer is going to get something to help him settle down."

Nahum looked up at the ceiling. David thought the man saw the light. Something in his eyes gave it away. The oldest of the men looked back at him. "There's nothing up there but cobwebs."

David started to say he'd never said the light was on the ceiling, but Ebenezer came in at that moment. He saw him uncork a small bottle that he recognized as the sleep dram. They planned to drug him again. He knew what he'd seen and what he'd heard.

"Open up." Ebenezer squeezed his jowls until his mouth opened.

The liquid filled up his mouth. The *doctor* closed his lips and held his mouth shut. Ebenezer rubbed his throat, forcing David to swallow the dram. Now God would be angry. He hoped that the Almighty would hold them accountable. Once he'd swallowed, Ebenezer let go of his mouth.

"The wrath of God will be upon you," David said.

He tried to struggle, but the drug worked fast. All his strength drained from him. His limbs went limp, and his lids slipped shut. All he saw was the purple light. The thrumming of it echoed through his head. The men let go of him. He willed himself to jump up and run, but the dram sucked everything from him.

"Is he out?" Marsh asked.

David felt his arm rise and fall. "Yes," Ebenezer said.

"Is he really crazy?" Nahum asked.

"Look up," Horace said. "What do you think?"

"He's not," Ebenezer said. "He's delirious from that damned light but not crazy."

"That light has never shown up in all the years we've celebrated Decoration Day," Nahum said.

"It's because he's the one. I am almost sure of it. No other preacher has ever been so affected by the place, and none has ever been so determined to work at our church," Marsh said. "I just hope that the light isn't too much for him."

Before he could hear the remainder of the conversation, David fell into deep sleep.

"Good morning."

David opened his eyes. Harsh, overpowering sunlight blinded him. He put his hand in front of his face to block the light. For a moment, David forgot where he was. He reached out for Anna, but his hand fell off the bed.

"Are you awake, Reverend Stanley?" Marsh said.

Reality set in. Anna was dead. He lay in a bedroom of a very creepy mansion in Tennessee, and God had talked to him last night. It had been more than that. God had beckoned him to join him. He sat straight up and stared his *host* dead in the face.

Marsh's steel-blue eyes looked hard and not very friendly. David wondered if the man's eyes had always looked so harsh. He couldn't remember. The thing he did remember was that Marsh and the other elders had kept him from meeting God.

"I want to leave," he said.

"Why?" Marsh's eyes softened to a look of curiosity.

"You kept me from God." David threw his feet off the bed and stood up.

A wave of dizziness washed over him. The room made a half whirl before he plopped back down on the bed. The springs creaked and popped under his weight. The wall tilted back the other way and finally stopped. The sun shining through the window seemed harsher. It stabbed his eyes and pierced his brain.

"What did that doctor give me?" he yelled, grasping his head as he did.

"The same sleep medicine that he gave you before."

"I don't believe you. You had me drugged. I heard you talking about me being the right one. What are going to do to me?"

Marsh walked around and sat on the edge of the bed. The mattress depressed. He suddenly had a very fatherly, worried look about him.

"I was going to let you preach," Marsh said, "but I'm beginning to reconsider it. I think you are losing grip on reality."

"The only thing I'm losing is my patience. Tell me what is going on."

"Ebenezer believes you are suffering from a kind of delirium. He believes that our isolation here has made it worse."

"Why isn't it affecting you?"

"Probably because we are used to the isolation. It is part of us," Marsh said. "It's in our character."

"How about the light?" David asked. "Is that part of the delirium, or is it God like I believe?"

"I think it's part of the delirium even though it started before the road ended up blocked. As for it being your God, I highly doubt that."

"Why? Don't you have faith?"

"I have faith in many things, Reverend, but I also know that you didn't hear your God's voice until you had another blow to the head. I find the two correlate."

"I'm not crazy," David said.

"I don't think you are, but I do think you've had two severe blows to the head that are affecting your judgment and rationality." Marsh stood. The mattress rose free of his added weight. "You will stay with me until Sunday. I don't want you back at the church. It has ill effects on you."

David knew he wasn't going to win this particular battle. Marsh owned the town as best he could tell. If Marsh didn't want David at the church, it wouldn't happen. Also, God had come to him in this room. He might do it again.

"I'll stay," he said.

"Are you going to cause any more excitement?"

"I'll try not to." As Marsh started out the door, David continued. "I left my sermon notes in the graveyard. I'm afraid they've been ruined by the weather, but could you fetch them?"

Marsh smiled. "I saw the pad out there when I found you unconscious in the church.

I brought it back with me. I'll have it sent up with some food."

"Thank you," he said and thought about all the canned goods. "Could I get some fresh fruit with it?"

"I don't think so. We don't have any. There's not enough time to eat up the surplus before Decoration Day." Marsh smiled and closed the door behind him.

"I've been hearing that a lot," David said.

The sun no longer blinded him. Clouds covered it so thickly that the light entering the room looked like twilight. Rain began to patter on the windows. David felt like he was living in a rain forest of some kind. Risking another wave of dizziness, he stood. His brain heaved forward and then backward but was not overcome with unsteadiness. He knelt by the bed, almost daring the demons of dizziness to overtake him. Everything pitched forward, toppling him face-first into the mattress, which was fitting since he planned such a position. While the world still moved in large loops, David began to pray.

"Our Father who is in heaven." David stopped and thought over his words. He wasn't making a public prayer but a private call of supplication. "My Father who is in heaven, hallowed be your matchless name. Oh Lord, hear me. Don't blame me for not coming to you last night. I was hindered in my way by forces beyond my control. You have called me to this place. Now stumbling blocks are before me everywhere. Give me guidance. Tell me what to do. Give me a sign. I need the reassurance that I am not losing my mind, and that you have given me a new calling and have revived my faith for the betterment. Protect against evils that hold back your powerful light. Free me from the nightmares and walking horrors like the woman with the octopus face. Oh Lord, give me a sign."

A tap came at the door. David looked up from his prayer. The sudden movement didn't send his brains reeling. Thomasine stepped inside, carrying a small tray with food and his legal pad on it. She placed the tray on the dresser and left without saying a word. David felt he might have gotten his sign. The woman bore a violet aura around her.

"In the name of your crucified Son, amen." He ended his prayer and stood.

The vertigo he'd experienced all the other times he'd stood was gone. He walked to the dresser without any trouble. A bowl of what looked like chicken salad sat on the tray with a few saltine crackers on a platter. Olives also garnished the meal. The ink on the legal pad looked undamaged by the weather. Both the lunch choice and the sermon cheered David.

"God to be praised," he said aloud.

He picked up his sermon notes and walked back to the bed. The chicken salad would be fine in a few minutes. He wanted to review his work. The fervor with which he had written yesterday undoubtedly had left the page full of brilliance. The beginning of the sermon read just as he remembered it. The time it had taken to pull those words from his mind gave them extra power. After half a page, the words became incomprehensible. They were not illegible. Each letter curled just so in dark ink. The letters themselves looked foreign, but not any language

David had ever seen. Despite the alienness of the letters, he recognized his handwriting.

A strong pull came from deep inside him. He walked to the window and looked out toward the church. Through a gap in the landscape he had never noticed before, the church's spire jutted upward. A violet aura surrounded it. Something as deep inside of him as that pulling told him the words would be translated there. The Holy Spirit lived there; David knew it. That great gift of God would provide translation.

Wooziness overtook him again. He stumbled back to the bed and collapsed there. The pages of his notepad crinkled beneath him as he passed out.

David screamed. The force of it tore through his throat, making it feel raw. After what seemed like an eternity of expelling the shriek, it broke off because his voice could take no more. The terror still clenched him. It took a long moment to realize what he screamed at. The woman in black stood at the foot of his bed. Her veil was piled on top of the large-brimmed hat she wore. The tentacles of her face reached out for him. She was like a strange Medusa who didn't turn men to stone but paralyzed them with terror.

His voice caught its second wind, and the scream blared out again. It took on the rhythm of a child wailing, a siren sound. The writhing appendages drew closer and closer to David's face. He almost felt the sharp suckers on his skin. The tentacles retracted, and the woman disappeared into a fog, like rich purple velvet.

The bedroom door slammed open. Marsh rushed in, wild-eyed, looking in all directions. Thomasine followed close behind him. She held a broom with the bristles up, poised to swat at whatever caused him to cry out.

"Are you okay?" Marsh asked, coming to his side.

"That was the woman with tentacles for a face." David knew he ranted. "She attacked me at the church the other night. That's why I fell and hit my head again."

Marsh pushed David back into a lying position. He examined the preacher's face. David looked into Marsh's eyes.

They had genuine concern in them. He felt the palm of one of Marsh's hands on his forehead and the back of his other hand on his cheek.

"Thomasine, get Thomas to fetch Ebenezer. Reverend Stanley is burning alive with fever. I am afraid it's boiling his brains."

"I'll get right on it," she said. "I'll bring up some ice too."

"With a washcloth and cool water as well," Marsh said. "We have to get this under control."

"I thought God gave me a sign of peace." David rose up and grabbed Marsh by the arm. He squeezed much harder than he intended to. The other man winced. "Why has he allowed this demon to come to me?"

"Lie back down," Marsh said. "You are getting more delirious due to the fever. You have to try and calm yourself."

"I have to leave this place before I lose everything," David said.

"You need to calm down." Marsh stood. "I'm going to get the ice and water. I can't wait on that dastardly slow Thomasine while she lollygags."

Marsh left the room, not closing the door after him. David felt happy about that. As long as he wasn't completely isolated, he had a shot of surviving. Any more time alone and that woman would do him in.

Bugs crawled under his skin. They itched. He scratched at them and felt his skin moving as they bored a path just under the top layer. They moved toward his face, toward his brain. Before they made it even to his elbow, he felt them boring into his cerebral cortex, making it look like Swiss cheese. A scream rose up in his throat but hung there.

Other things happened around him. At the seam between the molding and ceiling, the God light glowed down, but it was a faint, pastel lavender color. The sight worried him but not as much as what ran up the walls. Raised places milled around under the wallpaper. They looked like tentacles moving just beneath the surface. They sought a way free of the paper. A sudden realization came to David. He looked down at his arms, where the bugs crawled under his skin. Instead of seeing a scattering of small bumps sliding up his arms, veins appeared to move and slither toward his face. The tentacles crawled under his skin. The scream came free. He beat at his arms with a flattened palm as if trying to put out flames. He alternated the beatings from arm to arm in a spastic fit.

Marsh burst back into the room. He slammed a bowl on the dresser. Marsh grabbed David's wrists and pressed his arms to the bed. The man used remarkable strength. His appearance belied his ability.

"Thomasine, get in here now!" he said.

"Let me go!" David struggled. "The tentacles are heading toward my brain."

"What is the matter with him?" Thomasine asked in her usual flat tones. However, in David's near-crazed hearing, the words echoed.

"He's having a fit of some sort. Wrap some ice in that washcloth and get it on his forehead," Marsh said.

David struggled again to gain freedom from Marsh's grasp. He failed but laid his head down. Cooperation might give Marsh a reason to lessen his grip, and David could jump up and escape. He closed his eyes to feign calmness. The whole time the writhing tentacles moved in his arms. Marsh's hands stopped their progress for the moment, but the movement still felt maddening.

Thomasine placed the ice pack on his head. The pain of the sudden coldness stabbing into his brain radiated from David's forehead to his temples. The shock of it caused the writhing behind the wallpaper to stop. The squirming beneath his skin eased off as well. The weak glow continued right at the edge of the molding and the ceiling.

"That worked fast," Thomasine said.

"Good." Marsh sounded relieved.

David felt relief too. Clarity began to come back to his mind. He still felt the urge to run, but wouldn't. The sharp pain the cold pack brought to his head faded as well.

"I was afraid you were about to have a seizure," Marsh said to him.

He licked his lips. Terror left his mouth as dry as kindling. "I think I almost did."

Every word hurt as it came out. The screaming had ripped his throat raw. David smacked his lips in hopes that either Marsh or Thomasine would understand he wanted water.

"If I let go of your hands, are you going to stay still?" Marsh asked. David nodded his agreement. "I'll get you some water."

Marsh let go of David's hands. He moved them to bring back the circulation. All the excitement had caused them to go numb, but nothing seemed to crawl under the skin anymore. Marsh brought a cup of water. He put it to David's lips. The liquid felt like what the rich man begged Lazarus for from hell, a great relief.

"Bless you," David said. "I think I can hold the compress on my head."

Marsh nodded for Thomasine to let him. He pressed the cloth tighter to his head. The closer the ice cubes could get to the skin, the better. He closed his eyes. The faint glow on the ceiling was the last thing he saw. It seemed to brighten as he did so.

"Hopefully, Ebenezer will be here soon," Marsh said. "Stay still and keep your eyes closed. Thomasine and I will keep you company. Don't worry; we'll be quiet."

David was happy that they were staying. The creature seemed to fear Marsh. It disappeared as soon as it sensed him coming. Silence would also be welcome. His hearing seemed amplified. He was positive he could hear the rain hitting the oak leaves on the other side of the wall. As for now, David focused on the blackness behind his eyelids.

"Come along, Reverend Stanley," a friendly feminine voice said.

He opened his eyes. A raven-haired woman with porcelain-white features stared down at him. Sunlight lit everything. The addition of that wonderful natural light made the room much less oppressive. The woman didn't hurt things either. Her beauty was like nothing David had ever seen. It looked almost otherworldly. For a moment he felt that he might be looking at an angel beckoning him away from his dead body and taking him toward heaven.

"Am I dead?" he asked.

"No," she said. "I'm here to take you on a tour of our town. Alistair sent me to do so."

"Who are you?"

"That's not important."

"What day is it?" David sat up in bed. His head didn't swim. Nothing felt out of place.

"Monday," She put her hand out to him. "Come along. Time is wasting."

He got out of bed and took her hand. It felt soft, warm and welcoming. He hadn't held a woman's hand like that in quite a while. It made him miss Anna. They walked to the parlor downstairs. A little boy of about eight waited for them. He too had dark hair but vibrant blue eyes. David thought the boy looked like the son he'd wished he had, but God had not seen fit for him and Anna to have children. The boy smiled, full of life and boy vibrancy.

"This is my son," the woman said. "He'll be coming with us."

"What's your name?" David asked the youth.

"Boy," he replied with no guile whatsoever.

"Who's your daddy, Tarzan?" David laughed and looked at the woman. Neither reciprocated. They must not have gotten the joke.

"Are we ready?" she asked.

"Let's go," David said. "Will Thomas be driving us around?"

"We're going to walk. It's a very nice day." Boy took David's other hand.

The trio walked through the front door that opened by itself. The warmth of the sun radiated around him as they stepped onto the porch. The light washed out the entire image. Everything looked blanched. David wanted to shield his eyes, but had no need. The light didn't sting like he'd expected. The woman and Boy pulled him forward. They stepped off the porch onto the sidewalk. The town started to come into focus as the brightness of the light began to fade away.

David felt as if he floated down the street. He looked at his feet, but they disappeared into the white light. So did the woman's and Boy's. He allowed the two strangers to pull him down the hill into the heart of the town.

People walked down the street, normal-looking people.

None of them hunched over like toads. The café he'd seen days before looked brand new, gleaming with the light reflected off the windows. Patrons ate lunch and waved as they passed. He saw the library bustling with children. Sale advertisements hung in the window of the grocery store. The bright letters announced fresh ground chuck at $2.50 per pound, a good deal indeed. Across the creek that sparkled in the sunlight, a bright green starburst spun in the air of the gas station. Cars filled up, ready for a new day.

"What happened to this place?" David asked.

"You gave us this," the woman said. "You saved our town."

"What do you mean? How?"

"We can play again," Boy said. "It has been forever since we played."

The sound of giggling children filled up his ears. That was joined by the sound of laughing women, and then chuckling men. The joy of Innsboro swelled within David. Warmth like he'd never felt radiated from deep inside him. The light brightened again until it completely washed out everything. A cold gush of water hit him in the face.

David awoke to Ebenezer washing his face with an icy cloth. The room looked different. The ceiling was high and ornate. Scrolled moldings lined it. A gold chandelier dangled over the bed. Each bulb glowed with an orange filament. Water spattered on the window as it rained.

"Where am I?" he asked.

"In my bedroom," Marsh said, walking into his vision. "We decided to move you here for comfort."

"I was fine. The woman you sent to me walked me around town. It looked wonderful. Children played at the library, and folks ate lunch at the café. The sun beamed." He looked out the window at the rain streaking the glass. "What day is it?"

"Still Friday," Marsh said.

David turned to look at his host. A painting hung on the wall behind him. It was the portrait of the woman who had given him the tour. "She's the one who took me on the tour."

Marsh looked over his shoulder. "That's impossible. She's been dead for years.

She and a boy came into the room upstairs. They said you sent them." David feared he was starting to rant again. He didn't feel as well as he had only a few minutes ago.

"Was this the boy?" Marsh took a frame from the bedside table.

A small oil portrait of Boy stared at him. "I believe it is. He is a little bit younger in the painting."

"That is my son." Marsh pointed to the portrait on the wall. "That is my wife, Louisa. They could not have taken you on a tour."

"Fever dreams," Ebenezer said. "He probably drifted between waking and slumbering while we moved him. He saw the pictures, and they became part of the dream."

"It was real. I felt them. They said it was Monday and that I made everything better," David said.

"Lie back down." Ebenezer pushed on him. He put the cold cloth on his forehead. "I have something I want you to take."

"No more sleeping dram," Marsh said. "I think it's making things worse. He needs to be with us on Sunday."

David heard Ebenezer rattling in his bag. The old man held a plastic bottle up to his face to show him the medicine. David read the white block letters clearly: *Tylenol*. It was the first thing he'd recognized the whole time, and even in his fever stupor, he felt relief.

"This will break the fever yet." Ebenezer opened it and put the bottle to David's lips. "Drink until I tell you to stop."

"Don't give him too much," Marsh said.

"Let me be the doctor, Alistair."

The artificial cherry flavor filled up David's mouth. The bitter undertone of medicine lingered after he swallowed. By the time Ebenezer removed the bottle from his lips, a quarter of the liquid had gone into him.

"You'll feel better soon," Ebenezer said. "Sleep now and let the medicine work."

David agreed. He felt too sick and tired to argue. A sleep void of any dreams would be welcome. He began to snore but wasn't fully asleep yet.

"We have to do something else to stop it from completely

taking him before time," Ebenezer said. "What about some kind of religious talisman?"

"I found a cross around his neck before you got here," Marsh said on the other side of David's closed lids. "That wasn't keeping it away."

"What about one its symbols?" Ebenezer suggested.

A fist rapped on the headboard above David's head. He almost opened his eyes, but exhaustion kept him completely still. His hearing began to go in and out as sleep overwhelmed him.

"The bed has one carved into it," Marsh said. "I believe it protects me. Let's hope it does the same for him."

David heard nothing else of their conversation despite his efforts to hear more. Either exhaustion or the liquid Tylenol put him into a deep sleep.

SATURDAY

David walked beside Marsh, who held a large black umbrella over both of them. The rain pattered on the nylon material as they walked on the brick paths through the flower garden. Of everything in the whole town, David thought this place looked the most vibrant and fresh. Nothing of the stale dustiness of the town stayed in this place. Every single plant popped with color as if they had been colorized from some old black-and-white movie. He thought that might be exactly what it was. David knew he wasn't in a movie, but supposedly humans dreamed in black and white. Perhaps everything from the last week was a lengthy nightmare that fought to be in color. Only the flowers and the strange purple glow made the most of the toehold color took in his dream.

"I am sorry for walking in the rain," Marsh said. "Ebenezer said that you need to get fresh air to help you convalesce. If that fever is something more than just the aggravation of your concussion, I fear that this dampness will make things worse."

David looked back from one of the bright orange lilies blooming along the path. "I welcome the air. It feels good even if damp. Come to think of it, everything always seems damp around here. Why does it rain so much?"

"The geological nature of this valley," Marsh answered. "Supposedly cold water springs underlie this whole place. The creek in the center of town just bubbles up from the ground a few yards from the base of the mountain. Hot downdrafts cause all the moisture when they encounter that cold water."

"So does it rain this much in the winter?"

"I don't know."

David stopped walking. Marsh continued a few steps,

allowing the umbrella to quit shielding David from the rain. He walked back, covering them both again.

"How do you mean you don't know? Where do you go in the winter?"

"I go nowhere in the winter," Marsh said.

"Then why don't you know if it rains a lot?" David pressed.

"I wasn't listening to your question when you first asked it. I was hopelessly lost in other thoughts. Yes, it rains just as much in the wintertime."

"Where were your thoughts, Decoration Day?"

"How did you guess?"

"I've noticed that it is a very important day to the people of this town. Everyone uses it as a marker like New Year's Day. It's almost like it's a religious holiday."

"We need to keep walking. Doctor's orders." Marsh patted him on the shoulder to get him moving.

Both men ambled through the garden. They passed a bed of marigolds. The orange and yellows exploded with color like Fourth of July fireworks. The smell from the blooms wafted to David on the damp air. He couldn't remember such pungent marigolds. The smell reminded him of the hot summertime and his grandmother. He recognized all the flowers today, unlike the last time he visited the garden.

"Our past is important to us," Marsh said. "That is why we hold Decoration Day so dear."

David could still smell the marigolds. The smell almost spoke in the voice of his grandmother. He understood the importance of ancestors too. It still didn't answer the question about the particular day.

"What happens after Decoration Day?" he asked.

This time Marsh stopped walking, and David continued into the rain. The minister returned to the shelter of the umbrella. The other man stared at him as if some great question of the ages had been popped on him without any notice. David waited for the answer. Time passed with the tom-tom beating of the rain on the umbrella's fabric.

"Nothing," Marsh finally said. "Everything continues just as is."

"Why doesn't the grocery store order fresh food, then? Every time I ask, they say it is because the town cannot eat the surplus before Decoration Day. That tells me something changes on Monday," David said.

"I don't know," Marsh said. "You are asking questions that I cannot answer. All I can say is that it's the way it has always been done."

Frustration built up in David. Since he had been there, the town seemed to be keeping secrets and then blocking him from discovering them. He tired of the games and would put all his cards on the table.

"Something more is going on, Alistair. I haven't been dreaming, have I? Something comes to me at night and in the daylight. I've heard you and the others talking about how I am the one, and how this thing seems to like me. Tell me now what is going on."

"We should go back in before all this moisture negatively affects you," Marsh said.

"No. We stay here, and you answer my question." David grabbed hold of the other man's arm. He gripped it tightly enough to dig his fingernails into the skin.

"Our town is cursed," Marsh said. "We have been waiting for a preacher who can lift it."

"What do you mean?" David asked, keeping hold of Marsh's arm.

"We decorate the monuments to our ancestors to remember the Battle of Innsboro. They were massacred before the battle. We were so angry that the town elders petitioned a great power and sold the soul of the town to it for victory. It granted our petition, and we have been cursed ever since."

"The town sold its soul to the Devil?" David asked.

"Not to the Devil, to something far more powerful, an ancient thing that you cannot understand. The exposure you've had to it in spirit form has nearly killed you. That is why we are trying to keep you from it as long as possible. On Decoration Day, you will vanquish it, and we will be accursed no more."

"I'm a sacrifice?" David let go of Marsh's arm.

"No." The answer came quicker than David would have

liked. "According to the contract with the thing, a man of the One God will come and free us."

"So what happened to the preachers who haven't succeeded?"

"They leave," Marsh said.

"All I have to do is preach?"

"That's it. I think this great old thing is trying to stop you because you will break the contract. We've waited so long," Marsh said, almost looking excited.

"Why didn't you tell me this from the start?"

"You wouldn't have believed us. You'd have left as soon as you arrived. I knew last Sunday that you were different. Typically we put out an ad for a pastor a month before Decoration Day. Every other year one or two answer it. We take the more likely of the two. No one answered the advertisement this year, and then you came of your own will. The One God talks to you and tells you to save us."

David couldn't deny this, but Marsh implied the light was the thing holding the town enslaved. That couldn't be because God spoke from that light. He needed help, divine help. Prayer was the only answer.

"I need to pray about this," he said.

"We can go back inside," Marsh answered.

"I need to pray at the church."

"I don't think that is such a good idea. You are the most susceptible to the thing there. It is trying to stop you."

"I pray there, or I leave town. I'll walk up the mountain and climb over the rock fall."

Marsh looked at the ground. "So be it. If you will stay and try to help us, then I will oblige you, but wear this."

He reached in his pocket and brought out a necklace with a talisman on it. The small silver charm looked like the weird star at the church. Marsh handed it to David.

"What is this?" He took it and put it around his neck. The dreams and fever had been powerful, so if this small thing could ward it off, then David would use it.

"A fetish of the thing that curses us. The metal has protective powers. The shape is its symbol." Marsh pointed to the house. "Let's go back in, and I'll have Thomas return you to the church."

David knelt on a small wooden rail before the pulpit. A velvet cushion padded his knees against the hardness of the wood. He prayed. The words flowed from him. They weren't eloquent or elegant, just what he needed from God. The Lord had led him to this place. Now he'd discovered what the town wanted from him, but he needed more of what the Lord wanted for him. The revived evangelistic fire inside him sputtered with Marsh's revelation. He couldn't help feeling that, like Christ, he was the lamb being led to the slaughter. The prayer said all this and more. David ended with amen but remained kneeling where he was. Drops of sweat rolled down his back. The church pulsed with heat.

Until today, every time he'd entered the sanctuary, the place felt comfortable if not cool. The newfound heat seemed strange. This part of the building had no electricity, so no heating that didn't require someone to stoke a fire of some sort.

"Whew, if it ain't hot in here," Hester said from the back of the room.

David turned to see the frumpy maid walking down the aisle between pews. She fanned a rag in front of her face as she did. He stood to greet her.

"Why in blue blazes did you put the woodstove to heating?" she asked.

"I didn't. The place was like this when I got here," he said.

"Got to fix that. You've got water in that apartment, don't you?"

"Yes."

"Well, fill up the bucket I keep down behind the pulpit and bring it back for me to pour on the fire in the woodstove," she said. "We'll sweat off ten pounds in here if you don't. I just wonder who lit that thing."

"Perhaps it was an altar boy getting ready for tomorrow," David said, stepping onto the pulpit platform.

"What altar boys? We don't have any of those."

He stopped and looked at her. "Mr. Marsh told me that an altar boy would light the chandelier before services tomorrow."

"Don't know why he told you that. Ain't been any altar boys in years and years. I light the chandelier."

"Maybe he doesn't know that."

"Oh, he does. Sounds to me like he's lying to you. Hurry up with that water before I die of a heat stroke. I still got to tidy up a bit, and can't do it in a sweltering place like this."

David stepped down past the pit and found a tin bucket. He filled it from the sink in his bathroom and brought it back to Hester. The bucket sagged heavy in his hand. He figured she wouldn't be able to lift it, but she did. It was like she had no trouble with it at all. She disappeared somewhere on the other side of the pit. David heard the sizzle of water on hot embers, and the place filled up with the smell of wood smoke. Hester came out coughing and toting the bucket.

"Maybe you best go outside for a spell," she said. "Ain't raining or misting right now, and I heard you just got over a fever. This smell might throw you back into that fever, and tomorrow's the big day."

David welcomed getting away from that smell. He started down the aisle and stopped.

"Is it true the town is cursed?" he asked. "You're the only one who I believe has been completely honest."

"Yes, we're cursed."

"Am I a sacrifice?"

"Not that I know of. You're a preacher," she said, "and we ain't cursed like that."

"Thank you."

With his mind eased somewhat, David left the sanctuary and stepped into the cemetery. The air seemed drier even if the cloud cover stayed heavy. He didn't believe what Marsh had told him about the warm air and cold creek water. The curse kept it cloudy all the time. Why he believed in a curse, he didn't know, but somehow, he felt that God shared with him that it was the truth. A ray of sunshine was a lapse in the demon's grip on the town. He decided that if a ray broke through and illuminated him, then God answered his prayer in the affirmative.

He walked toward the headstone the woman from his nightmare had stood before. The stone read the same. The boy's beside it did as well. Now David wondered about the years on the stones. He couldn't figure out why they would be dated so far back in time. The town put so much emphasis on Decoration Day because of the curse. Perhaps all time in their minds stayed focused on the 1800s. He'd never heard of such behavior, but that didn't mean it could exist.

As he scanned the graves, a beam of sunlight broke through the clouds. It landed on a stone near the back wall where he'd climbed over to get the wildflowers. David had his sign from God. He was supposed to save the people. Tomorrow his sermon would dispel the clouds of these people's curse. They would be free to celebrate their lives instead of remembering the dead and having only that one day to look forward to. He walked to where the light landed. The stone read *Alistair Marsh, 1828*

The sunlight faded. David knew the demon curse fought back against him when the rain began to fall thick and cold. He expected to see it roll off his skin in purple drops, but it only looked like rain. However, the talisman that he had placed under his shirt grew hot. The thing that cursed the town wanted to get to him, but the charm spread its protection around him. The One God, as Marsh had called the Almighty, protected him.

SUNDAY: DECORATION DAY

David stayed up far too long. His watch had quit working the day his car encountered the purple mist, but he always kept a windup spare primed and ready. According to this gold-tone timepiece, early Sunday morning wore on. He'd spent the time finishing up his sermon. As he'd thought when he found the strange writing on the pad, the letters made sense when he got back to the church. God saw fit for him to have glossolalia. David had never heard of someone writing in tongues, but God worked in mysterious ways.

The sections he hadn't been able to read turned out to be about the dangers of ancestor worship. Once he'd reviewed his work, the words flowed out of him again. God must have guided his pen, because David knew he would never have been able to write so quickly. The Bible verses came to him without looking up a single one or using the concordance he'd had since seminary. The verses were good. This congregation wouldn't know what hit them, and hopefully the demon that cursed the town wouldn't either. David knew that thing tried to get to him. The charm around his neck heated up several times. Once, around midnight, it took on a faint purple glow.

As he put the final touches on his sermon, David felt his eyelids slip down. In the morning, he'd need everything in him preach the word of God and free the people of Innsboro. For that to occur, he needed to get deep rest. After all the turmoil of the fever and taunts of the cursed demon, deep sleep would be deeply welcomed.

The morning broke to the sound of thunder. David sat up in bed as the noise rumbled overhead and echoed down the side of the mountain. The reverberation shook his apartment and probably the whole church.

He got out of bed and walked to the small window. Although it faced the mountain, David saw a slip of the sky. Dark clouds hung there, ready to drop a massive amount of rain. Lightning streaked from cloud to cloud in yellow zigzags. The thunder followed right on top. The storm sat dead over the valley, but not a drop of rain fell.

David worried the storm would hinder the congregation from attending service. The talisman around his neck heated up again in sync with another shaking thunderclap. It was like the whole sky tore open. He wondered if it might be the rapture. The whole time he'd been pondering over what Marsh and Hester told him, he'd never thought that he might be fighting against the Antichrist and bringing about the end of days.

"Don't flatter yourself," a familiar voice said.

He turned around and saw Anna standing behind him near the stove. She wore a flowing white gown like an angel might wear.

"How are you here?" he asked her.

"I just am. This isn't the rapture," she said. "Don't let this vision of me make you think differently. It's just a lightning storm, nothing more."

"But Marsh said he thinks I can free them of a curse," David said.

"When did the man I married become so superstitious? There is no curse."

"What about all the strange things that have been happening to me?"

"Hallucinations, nightmares. Maybe you're going crazy," she said.

David began to think that this apparition sounded less and less like his wife. Just a few nights ago, she had tried to protect him.

"I think I should still preach to these people all the same."

"Take off that silly charm then. It's an idol, you know. The One God doesn't like idols."

He looked down at his chest where the medallion rested under his shirt. Although the fetish didn't feel warm, it glowed with that eerie nightmare light.

"No."

Anna lunged for him. Her face transformed into a wad of writhing tentacles as she did so. David stepped back, but as soon as her hands touched the cloth of his shirt, the apparition dissipated into lavender mist. He caught a scream in his throat and let it out as a long sigh.

The door to his apartment opened. Marsh stepped inside. He looked David up and down.

"There isn't much time, Reverend Stanley. I think you better put on your vestments or whatever."

"It's still early," David answered.

"It is a quarter until ten," Marsh said. "The congregation is almost completely gathered."

David looked around. Nothing in his apartment had changed, but the thunder no longer rolled, and his watch told him it had been two hours since he jumped out of bed expecting to see four horsemen. The encounter with the demonic version of Anna had drained hours from his day. This demon was powerful and determined.

Not wanting to waste another minute, David pulled his long vestment robe over his pajamas. Nothing of the plaid trousers could be seen. He slipped on his loafers and grabbed his notes and Bible as he left the apartment.

The sanctuary hummed with mumbled conversation. It felt alive even though he couldn't see it yet. The pit beside the steps that led to the podium platform looked almost cheery. When he stood on the platform, he saw the small auditorium had around fifty or sixty people in the pews. They crammed close to each other toward the front. The elders, without any wives, sat at the very front. The rest of the pews appeared to be filled with the servants; numerous bulbous, watery eyes looked up at him. The whispers continued.

Marsh sat on a short pew to the side of the stage. He patted the narrow, empty seat beside him. David took it, pulling his robe down to make sure it hid his pants.

"Are you ready?" Marsh asked.

"Is this everyone?" David answered.

"The whole town."

"But the population sign..."

"Is wrong," Marsh finished the sentence. "I will begin by leading the congregation in a few songs. Then you can start. Is that okay?"

"No prayer or Scripture reading?" David asked.

"That's your job."

Marsh reached under the bench and brought out a small hymnal. He approached the podium while thumbing through the book. David felt beneath the bench for another book, but didn't find one. Fortunately, he knew many sacred songs and would be able to wing it. Preachers were expected to be good orators, not choirmasters.

"Everyone, turn to song forty-two in your hymnals," Marsh said.

David heard the familiar and slightly heady sound of hymnals being pulled from the holders on the pews and of the pages turning. Showtime had arrived. Butterflies flew in his stomach. It had been so long since he'd preached a sermon that he hoped he still could.

The song started. He recognized the tune of "Let the Lower Lights Be Burning" and opened his mouth to sing. The words sounded different. The crowd slurred and rolled syllables nothing like English. The language was nothing David had ever heard. He imagined it would be what the words on his pad would sound like if spoken. God had given him the ability to read it, but had neglected the ability to translate the spoken words.

He flipped his pad over to the side with writing. The first half of the first page read in English. The rest was in that mysterious language. He turned to the next page. More of the same strange writing was scrawled out in black ink. Nothing was readable. The butterflies quit flying around and started slamming into the pit of his stomach.

David kept turning pages and finding the same thing. Panic gripped him. The song ended and a new one began. The tune was

"Nearer My God to Thee." Soon he'd be giving a sermon from words he didn't know. The words remained alien. He clutched at his chest as it tightened with panic. Through the thickness of the robe and his underlying shirt, the stems radiating off the charm poked his fingers. Perhaps God would not allow him to preach his Word wearing a symbol related to a demon.

He worked his arm into his robe and grabbed the charm. The thin chain snapped easily when he pulled it. He brought the fetish out and tossed it into the pit without thinking that he might need it or that Marsh might want it back.

Sweat beaded around his temples, and a drop rolled down his back. He looked at the words on the page. They remained the same. The song became clear though. He heard the lyrics in English, and they matched those he remembered of the song. David began to sing along. He somehow knew that it was in the strange tongue. The song ended.

"Now, Reverend Stanley will present us a sermon on this, the 148th Decoration Day."

Marsh stepped aside. David took his notes, still in the strange language, and stood at the podium. Fortunately, he knew the verse he would open with. Maybe God would see fit for him to read his notes soon.

"Ladies and gentlemen, I know this is an important day for you because of your history, but let me warn you of worshipping ancestors and the dead. Ecclesiastes 9:5 says: *For the living know that they shall die: but the dead know not any thing, neither have they any more a reward; for the memory of them is forgotten.*"

He looked at his notes. The words became readable. David started to preach as if it was a hellfire and brimstone sermon. The room heated up. More sweat rolled down his back and his cheeks. He paused for effect and noticed that the congregation seemed to sweat as well. They remained still and quiet though. The look they gave him might have been called awestruck. David had never seen the expression. All he knew was that he liked the attentiveness.

His breath caught, he continued. Sweat dripped into his eyes. It stung. He would have wiped it away, but he didn't want to mess up his tempo. A realization came over him as he flipped the page on his notepad. The air felt sultry like a swamp on a hot July day. The audience's faces had changed as well. The awestruck gape to their mouths was now one of restrained terror. Every gaze focused on a point behind him.

David stopped his sermon. A noise like a wet growl rumbled behind him. He turned to look out the windows. Drops of violet rain rolled down the glass, thick like molten lead. The crowd began to sing. He couldn't recognize the words, but the tune was that of "Dixie." The heavy rain washed down the windows now. The color darkened the panes so that the light coming in seemed to shine through stained glass. David noticed that despite the downpour, the sun shone brightly.

He turned around to face the pit, knowing full well that whatever terrified the audience came out of it. The dread of the horrible hole that he'd had since encountering it the first time came to full fruition. As he glanced toward it, a thing jutted from the pit, so horrible it took the scream from his throat.

The globular creature dangled over the abyss by two long tentacles balanced on the edges of the stonework. The thing took up most of the space over the pit. More of the hideous appendages flailed at the air. A mouth full of rows of teeth took up a large portion of the front of the globular body. Bright, pulsing lavender light shone from beneath it.

David realized that the symbol on the steeple and the gate wasn't some kind of star, but an idol of this thing that had cursed the town. All he could wonder was how many other ministers had greeted the creature over the last century and a half.

The congregation's song swelled as a tentacle reached for him. He tried to flee but could not. God spoke to him at that moment. The One God told him to stand fast in the face of evil. The tentacle wrapped around him and lifted him in the air. The crowd cheered. He thought he heard a prayer or two mixed in before the creature shoved him into its horrible mouth.

The teeth didn't tear him to shreds; instead, he plummeted into great, unknown depths. Knowledge found him there. He saw everything and understood. A band of Union marauders came to Innsboro while the men and servants were away. They slaughtered the old, the women, and the children. Marsh found his dead son and wife, Boy and the woman from David's fever dream, and swore revenge. He sold the town to the creature in exchange for defeat of the Union forces that had massacred his family. An army of toad men like the ones David saw the night the purple rain first fell rose up and defeated the soldiers. Marsh led them to victory. After that, the town owed its soul to the creature. It gave them an out: to find a holy man of the One God to take their place. The man would not be afraid to preach the truth. Once this preacher was found, the town would be free. Until that time of deliverance, the town would disappear, only to reappear long enough to find a preacher, celebrate Decoration Day, and then go back to the abyss, where the inhabitants lived on and waited. Some died after a long time. Others, mostly the servants, slowly turned into the toad people

David watched other preachers destroyed by the creature as the years passed. He saw the creature watching him come down the road with dread and anticipation of his sermon. The creature reviled him for his ability to break the contract, but at the same time desired him for its own evil purposes. A purple haze rose over all this, and all knowing faded out.

MONDAY

David awoke in a green field. Yellow wildflowers bloomed on the side of the hill. His car sat parked on the side of a rutted mountain road. He brushed off his pants and headed to his car. The drive up the mountain was easy. Happiness filled him up because he had done what God wanted him to do. Now he was the missionary to new people, and God resided in his brain. His long tentacles wound around His blobby body, floating in a purple smoke, biding His time until He could be worshipped again.

ABOUT THE AUTHOR

Vic Kerry lives in Alabama with his wife, four dogs, and two cats. He has an MFA in writing popular fiction from Seton Hill University and is haunted by the ghost of his dearly departed Lovecraft-loving cat, Possum H. Puss Lovecraff. You can like him or friend him on Facebook or stalk him through Twitter and Instagram.

Curious about other Crossroad Press books?
Stop by our site:
http://store.crossroadpress.com
We offer quality writing
in digital, audio, and print formats.

Enter the code FIRSTBOOK
to get 20% off your first order from our store!
Stop by today!